# THE NEIGHBORHOOD

Luis —

Enjoy The Neighborhood

Edwin Budget

## Other Books by Erina Bridget Ring

*Knit 2, Purl 2, Kill 2, A Caretaker's Story of Survival*

*Breakfast with the FBI*

*Diapers, Drama, and Deceit: The Mothers of Easthaven*

*Writing Ain't for Sissies*

# THE NEIGHBORHOOD

By

ERINA BRIDGET RING

*The Neighborhood is a work of fiction. Names, characters, places, and incidents are products of the writer's imagination or have been used fictitiously and are not to be construed as real. Any resemblances to persons living or dead, actual events, places, incidents, or organizations is coincidental.*

ISBN-13: 978-0-692-14184-7

ISBN-10: 0-692-14184-7

Cover design by Rae Monet

Edited by Carolyn Woolston

Formatted by Concierge Self-Publishing

(www.ConciergeSelfPublishing.com)

# Dedication

*For my husband, Jack*

# Acknowledgments

I would like to thank my family and my friends who gave their support, especially Lincoln Beals, Paula Philipps, Barbara Heppe, Doris Gentry, Lisa Winograde, Kyle Frasure, Lisa Averill, Dave Sawyer, and David Woolston. Finally, thanks to my editor and friend Carolyn Woolston, without whose expertise my stories would not have made it onto the printed page.

.

# Foreword

Many years ago when I was young, I lived in the state of Indiana. It was a time in my life when I could roam freely after school and investigate my neighborhood, which was in a quiet subdivision. I remember that I had a friend a few streets over whose father was a big game trophy hunter. He drove an old beat-up pickup truck with a rifle mounted in the back window. Their house had an eerie feel to it from the minute you walked through the front door. I was fascinated by the stuffed turkey in the glass case in the hallway and terrified of the huge black stuffed bear standing in the corner. And I never forgot the eyes of all those animals he'd shot; the heads hung on the walls, perched on dressers, and stood in corners. One even sat in the middle of the dining room table!

I had another friend whose mother was always competing in beauty pageants and was grooming her daughter to do the same. I always remembered how elegantly they both dressed, and how they wore their tiaras on special occasions.

When I came up with the idea for this book, I dug into my memories of neighborhoods where I had lived years ago—in the South, in big cities on the East Coast, in small Midwestern towns—and I kept what I found interesting.

And over the years I learned something. It doesn't matter where you live because basically all people are the same. All of us live in the same neighborhood!

I hope you enjoy this book; it's a work of fiction based on my recollections of neighborhoods I lived in when I was young.

Erina Bridget Ring

Napa, California

2018

Chapter One

# The Neighborhood

The neighborhood was called Sherwood Forest. Located in the small town of Shellville, the area had lush, grassy green parks and hundred-year-old elm trees lining the streets, which were named Robin Hood Boulevard, Little John Way, Maid Marian Street, and Sir Richard Road. Each home was well kept, tastefully painted cream with white trim or beige with darker trim, and each sported at least one BMW, Lexus, or Camry in the driveway.

Gretchen and Jarrod woke up in their new home at 28 Sir Richard Road on a crisp October morning and gazed at the welter of moving cartons and furniture the movers had unloaded the previous day. It was a quiet neighborhood of seven tri-level homes in a cul-de-sac with a large empty lot at the end of the street. At least they had thought it was quiet when they bought the house in September.

Gretchen pulled her robe on over her pink nightgown and walked into the sunny kitchen, which was on the second level. Mr. Parker was nipping at her feet. "Parker, not now!" She bent to scratch behind his ears. "Don't give me that look, you silly dog. I'll walk you later, after I have some coffee." The fluffy brown Yorkshire terrier padded over to his bed in the corner of the kitchen and plopped down.

Gretchen studied the packing boxes, but try as she might she couldn't find the carton with the coffeemaker in it. Or the coffee.

"Jarrod," she called. "We should go out for breakfast. I need a cup of coffee before I can face unpacking."

"Okay," her husband said. "Let's go right away so I can start putting together my workbench in the garage."

She sighed and stared at the sea of boxes. *The garage? He's worried about the garage?*

"Honey, I'm sure it'll be a nice workbench area for all those projects you have in mind, but after driving five hundred miles from Lafayette yesterday, I really need some coffee."

They drove to Strudel's Bakery, a few blocks from their house. Next door, Gretchen spied a bookstore. "After we unpack, I want to check that out."

"Sure, honey. You buy some more books. I'll find a hardware store and buy some more tools."

After a quick breakfast of coffee and apple strudel, Jarrod went down to the garage and Gretchen headed for the kitchen. She had just opened a big carton of dishes when the doorbell rang. "Coming," she called. She rushed down the stairs and almost tripped over a box of books.

A sharp twinge in her neck shot all the way down to her lower back, and she gritted her teeth.

"Take your time," a woman's voice called.

Mr. Parker appeared at Gretchen's feet as she opened the door. Before her stood a woman with perfectly coiffed flame-red hair wearing a sheer low-necked blouse, skinny jeans, and wedge sandals. Beautiful diamond earrings dangled from her ears, and a diamond-studded cross hung on a long gold chain between her breasts.

*Oh, heavens, our first visitors already!*

"Good morning," Gretchen said with a smile.

"Hi, there," the woman said. "I'm your next-door neighbor." The terrier growled.

"Is your dog friendly?"

"Usually, yes. I don't know what's gotten into him this morning. He never growls."

Gretchen extended her hand, but the woman ignored it and pushed past her into the foyer. "I'm Maggie. I came to help you unpack."

"Really, that's not necessary," Gretchen said. But before she could say another word, Maggie dove into a carton and began unwrapping a plate. She wore a diamond watch and an infinity bracelet on the same wrist.

Gretchen tugged at her loose tee shirt and sensible denim jeans and absentmindedly smoothed one hand over her hair. Then she remembered she'd kicked off her loafers after breakfast and her feet were bare.

"I've lived here ever since all these houses were built four years ago," Maggie announced, lifting out another plate. "Actually, ours was the first house built."

"That's nice, Maggie. And it's good to meet you, but I really don't need any help this morning." She reached to take the unwrapped plate out of her hand and noticed that Maggie wore the biggest diamond ring she had ever seen.

"Oh, it's no problem at all," Maggie said. She tugged the plate free of the bubble wrap and turned it over to check the maker. "Ah, Lenox," she murmured. "Nice."

Gretchen tightened her lips. She didn't want Maggie inspecting her plates or anything else. She stepped in front of her to block her access to the carton of china, but the woman pivoted away to set the unwrapped plate in the cupboard beside the sink.

"Oh, no," Gretchen protested. "I'm not putting my plates there."

Maggie just looked at her. "That's where we *all* store our plates," she said.

Gretchen frowned. "Really? Everyone in this neighborhood

stores their plates in the same cupboard?"

"Oh, yes. We all have the same floor plan and our kitchens are all the same." She grabbed another plate and began to unwrap it.

*What is this woman doing touching my plates? In my house? Telling me where to put my dishes?* She took a deep breath and caught sight of Jarrod in the kitchen doorway with Mr. Parker at his feet.

"Hello," her husband said, directing a smile at Maggie.

Maggie looked up. "Hi. I'm Maggie. My husband Chet and I live next door at number twenty-six. We have the custom grey wavy cement driveway. It's the latest décor for driveways!" she exclaimed. "We also have beautiful custom French doors throughout the house. I had them shipped all the way from Europe."

Jarrod stared at her. "Gretchen, I need to go to the hardware store. Do you need anything?"

Gretchen shook her head. *The only thing I need is for you to walk this woman out of our house!* She sent him a desperate look, but Jarrod just nodded. "See you later, honey. Nice meeting you, Maggie," he said politely.

Maggie bent over the carton of china. "Gretchen, I think you should put your cups and glasses in this cupboard." She pointed to the shelves next to the refrigerator.

Gretchen gritted her teeth. "Maggie, I'll think about it, but right now I'm going to walk you out." She took the woman's elbow and escorted her out of the kitchen and down the stairs. "I have things I have to do. When I'm finished unpacking, maybe we could have coffee sometime, okay?"

Maggie clasped her hands at her waist. "Really, I have all the time in the world to help you today."

Gretchen tried to smile. "Thanks, Maggie, but I really have some things to do, and I need to see what works for me in my kitchen." She put a slight emphasis on "my."

Maggie sighed, then took a folded paper out of her jean pocket. "Here's a list of everyone's home phone and cell phone numbers, our addresses, and next of kin."

She hid her surprise. *Next of kin? What went on in this*

*neighborhood that people would need this information?*

"That's nice of you, Maggie," she managed, taking the list. Mr. Parker started to bark, and Gretchen bent to grab his collar as she reached to open the front door.

"Wait," Maggie said. "What are your phone numbers? I'll update all the neighbors."

"Maybe later. We'll be changing our phone numbers." She pulled the door open, but Maggie stopped and studied it. "You need to go to the florist and have a wreath made for your door. You'll find the florist next to Shellville Bookstore at the far end of Robin Hood Boulevard."

"Thank you," Gretchen said. She closed the door and stood stock still for a moment. Were all the neighbors here this friendly?

For the next four hours she worked unpacking the rest of the china and the kitchen utensils. When she finished, Jarrod walked up from the garage. "Ready for a break?"

"Yes! My back is killing me! What do you have in mind?"

"Dinner out at some restaurant called Maria's Kitchen. Our

new neighbor, Chet, spent all afternoon in the garage with me, rearranging my workbench. I was really pissed, and now I'm starving."

Gretchen laughed. "I'd say Maggie and Chet are being over-helpful, wouldn't you?"

"I hope the rest of the neighbors aren't like that. Chet got to be really annoying after a while."

\*     \*     \*

Two hours later, when they were leaving Maria's Kitchen, Chet and Maggie walked in. "Oh, stay and have a drink with us," Maggie invited.

Gretchen looked at Jarrod. From the look on his face, she knew he just wanted to go home. "Another time, all right? We need to get home to our dog."

Suddenly Maggie yelled to the back of the restaurant. "Maria! Come and meet our new neighbors."

A harried-looking older woman in a food-stained apron appeared. "So, you are Gretchen and Jarrod? What is your last name?"

"O'Malley," Jarrod said. He turned toward the door.

Maggie grinned at her. *Her teeth are so white they look unreal!*

"Where do you work, Jarrod?" Maria asked.

"I own my own business."

"Here in town?" she pursued.

"Yes." But Maria wouldn't let it go.

"Do you employ a lot of people?"

Jarrod took Gretchen's elbow. "It's been a long day, and we have a lot of unpacking to do." They walked to their car in silence.

"Wow!" he said when they climbed into the black Lexus. "Maria is just as nosy as Maggie and Chet. They want to know everything about us!"

"Maybe it's because we're new. They just want to get to know us."

"You got that right, honey!" He let out a long breath. "Chet drilled holes in our garage wall, can you believe that? He didn't ask me if I wanted my pegboard where he put it. I didn't notice until it was too late. I tried to shoo him out, but it was weird. He touched each one of my tools, and he was really interested in the old ones I inherited from Dad.

"Maggie unwrapped our plates and tried to tell me which cupboard to put them in."

"Weird," Jarrod muttered.

They drove the rest of the way in silence.

Chapter Two

## Rise and Shine

The doorbell rang at 6:30 the next morning.

Jarrod groaned and rolled over. "Oh, shoot, who could that be at this hour?"

Gretchen pulled on her robe, walked to the front door, and peeked through the security lens. Maggie!

Slowly she opened the door. "Hello, Maggie. Forgive me if I don't invite you in; I'm still in my robe."

"Gretchen, I've brought coffee and some homemade muffins for you and Jarrod. Time to get up and unpack those boxes! I've come to help you."

Gretchen stifled a yawn. *Is she kidding?* "Maggie, that's really sweet of you, but that won't be necessary. But thanks so much for the coffee and muffins."

Maggie's thin eyebrows rose. "The coffee beans are from

Shellville Roasting Company and the blueberries in the muffins are from my own garden. And . . ." She pulled something out of a bag. "I made these napkins for you and embroidered your initials on them."

All at once Gretchen felt awful for refusing the woman's offer of help, even if it was 6:30 in the morning. "Maggie, maybe you could help me this afternoon, say around two?"

"Oh, I'd love to. I could come even earlier if you like." She looked at Gretchen expectantly.

"No, this afternoon would be fine. I'll see you then." She closed the door and went back into the bedroom.

"Who was that so early in the morning?" Jarrod asked.

"Maggie."

"At this hour?"

Gretchen let out a long sigh. "She brought coffee and homemade muffins. And . . ." She rolled her eyes. " . . . of all things, she embroidered our initials on some napkins she'd made."

Mr. Parker yawned and rolled over in his crate.

"You know something, Jarrod? I think we're living next door to Martha Stewart! I can only imagine what Maggie's house looks like inside."

"I'm not the least bit curious, are you?"

"Not only that," she added, "I felt I had to invite her back to help me this afternoon."

Jarrod chuckled. "Really? After she touched your wedding china?"

"Well, yes."

"Better keep an eye on her, honey."

Gretchen dressed quickly and went into the kitchen, stepping around the jumble of unpacked cartons. She found two cups and was filling them with coffee when an odd feeling settled over her. She looked up and saw that something across the street was moving. "Jarrod, look! The blinds on that house across the street are jiggling."

"Huh?"

"Yes, just watch. Someone is staring at us out their window. See how the slats on the blinds are moving?"

Mr. Parker's ears lifted.

Jarrod peered out, then returned to his coffee. "Well, it's their house, right? Whoever it is can look out their window if they want."

"Well, yes, it is their house, but don't you think it's kind of nosy to watch us?"

"Yeah, maybe."

Gretchen studied her husband. "Well *I* think it's nosy. It's a good thing the interior decorator is coming tomorrow to measure our front windows for curtains."

Chapter Three

## Getting To Know You

The next morning the interior window designer, Marcia Bloomquist from Bloomquist Decorators, arrived. Gretchen showed her first to the master bedroom where a window covering was needed immediately. Then Marcia walked from room to room with her clipboard and tape measure while Gretchen asked her advice about blinds and window treatments. In the middle of deciding on color schemes for each room, the front doorbell rang.

"Maggie!" Gretchen smiled, even though she was surprised.

"I'm here early," Maggie said. I hope you don't mind." She wore a royal blue silk blouse tucked into tight denim jeans, a pair of royal blue high heels, and a diamond clip in her long, wavy red hair.

Gretchen tugged at her worn tee-shirt. "Well, yes, you are

early. I haven't had lunch yet. My decorator is measuring our windows."

"Oooh," Maggie squealed. "Let me see what you're doing in all your rooms."

Before Gretchen could stop her, Maggie was marching into the kitchen, where the decorator had just finished measuring the window over the sink and was moving toward the basement stairs.

"Maggie, wait."

Too late.

"Hi, I'm Maggie, Gretchen's neighbor."

The decorator held her clipboard out to Gretchen. "I need your signature," she said. "I'll bring your bedroom drapes over as soon as they arrive."

Gretchen signed the paper and showed the decorator out. When she closed the door she looked up to see Maggie staring at her kitchen cabinets. "I like where you put your plates and glasses," she said.

Gretchen jerked. "You didn't look in my cupboards, did

you?" Mr. Parker growled at her.

No answer. Suddenly all she wanted to do was get Maggie out of her house. "How about we go over to the coffee shop for a bite to eat?"

"Sure," Maggie said. On the way to the garage, Maggie studied all the packing boxes in the basement. "What a mess!" she exclaimed.

Gretchen frowned. "Maggie, we just moved in." She tried not to sound irritated, but the truth was she thought her neighbor was not only nosy but critical. The minute she backed the black Lexus out of the driveway, Maggie started talking.

"We're a really close-knit neighborhood," she said. "Everybody knows everybody else, and we all get along really well."

Gretchen just looked at her, then made a right turn onto Robin Hood Boulevard.

"You and Jarrod have to keep this Sunday free," Maggie said as they walked into Strudel Bakery.

"Oh? Why is that?"

"We're having a welcoming party for you and Jarrod. It's at my house. Six o'clock. We'll keep the dress code casual this time."

Gretchen raised her eyebrows. *Dress code? For a neighborhood gathering?* She looked for a table for two.

"Your kitchen looks great," Maggie said as they sat down. "I'm going right home and change my china and glassware exactly the way you have yours."

Gretchen looked at her. "Why would you do that?"

"It looks more functional. I've decided to get all new plates and glasses. And I'm having custom doors put on all my cupboards.

"But your house is new. Why would you want to remodel your kitchen cupboards?"

"Oh," Maggie said "I just got a big settlement and I have money to play with. I can do whatever I want."

Gretchen could think of nothing to say to that, so she ordered a chicken sandwich and kept quiet while Maggie talked.

"Reilly and Dorothy Hogan live on the other side of your

house," she confided. "Reilly is a deer hunter. Dorothy tells everyone she's a nurse, but she's really just a receptionist." She rolled her eyes. "Can you imagine? She says she has all sorts of degrees, but she ends up being just a receptionist."

Gretchen began to squirm. *What an unkind thing to say! Such information was none of her business.*

"If I want to find out who's sick," Maggie went on, "I ask Dorothy. She knows everything about everyone, and she talks."

"How could she know so much if she's just the receptionist for one doctor?" Gretchen said glumly.

"She has a computer link connecting all the medical specialists in town."

Gretchen put her sandwich down. "Which doctor does Dorothy work for?"

Maggie thought for a moment. "She works for Dr. Ruggiero."

After a moment she went on. "Then there's Marie and Darrell Levine at 30 Sir Richard Road. They're really religious and stay pretty much to themselves. They don't drink, and we'll be serving cocktails at the party, so they may not come."

Gretchen took a bite of her sandwich. Not only did Maggie notice everything about their neighbors, she spread it around!

"Let's see," Maggie went on, "Katalie and Gian Carlo DeCarrio live next to the Levines. We call them Ken and Barbie."

Gretchen managed to keep a straight face. *Maggie is so critical!*

"They're nice," Maggie continued, "but Katalie thinks she's smarter and prettier than everyone else. She and Gian Carlo have a real assortment of people living at their house. Not all at the same time, of course; they come and go. Mostly European people," she added.

Gretchen stopped chewing. "Can they do that in our neighborhood? Rent out rooms?"

Maggie inched her chair closer. "No. Our neighborhood isn't zoned for that." She folded her arms. "I've called the police twice about it. It's just a matter of time before we get rid of them and those awful cars they park on the street. It's bad enough that the Hogans park their big Ram truck in their driveway backwards. You'd think they would know this isn't that kind of neighborhood."

Gretchen stared at her. *Since when can't people park backwards in their own driveway?*

"Larry and Lucille Stanley live across the street and down from you." Maggie sighed dramatically. "Let's just say you don't want any of their children coming into your house."

"Why not?"

Maggie leaned across the table. "Their adult children live with them, and they're all felons." she whispered. "Felons!"

"What? How do you know that?"

"Oh, I just know. You need to stay away from them. We had a block party a few years ago, and someone caught one of the boys going through our medicine cabinets."

*This is bizarre,* Gretchen thought. *Is Maggie being truthful or just making things up?*

Her neighbor rattled on. "Then directly across from you is Tad Sabbin. His wife's name is Dana, and she lives around the corner on Little John Way."

"They live in two separate houses?"

"They just can't get along," Maggie said. "They stay married, but they have separate houses and separate lives. Their children move back and forth between them. You should hear them yell at each other. One day I was standing out in front and I could hear them two houses away!"

"Wow," Gretchen murmured. *This neighborhood is sounding odder and odder.*

Maggie suddenly focused her attention on Gretchen. "What about you and Jarrod?"

"What do you mean?"

"Oh, come on," Maggie coaxed. "Tell me about you two."

Gretchen worked to keep smiling. "Well, we moved here to be closer to our parents now that they're getting older."

"Oh?" Maggie waited expectantly.

Gretchen pointedly looked at her watch. "My goodness, look at the time! Maggie, I need to drop you off. I have an appointment in thirty minutes."

Her face changed. "Can't I help you organize your home?"

"I'm sorry, Maggie. Not today."

On the drive back, Maggie talked nonstop about her custom-made cupboards "made from medium-beige hardwood with brass fixtures," and Gretchen nodded and um-hmmed until they reached their neighborhood.

"Who's your appointment with?" Maggie asked as Gretchen parked the car.

"The locksmith."

Maggie looked at her sideways. "Why do you need a locksmith?"

"Whenever we move into a new house we always change the locks."

"Really? I'll have to tell Chet. Maybe we should change our locks, too."

Chapter Four

## Welcome to the Neighborhood

"Wow, honey, it smells amazing in here!"

Gretchen slapped her husband's hand away from her fresh-baked apple pie. "Don't pick at the crust, Jarrod. It's for the party, and it has to look perfect."

"Kinda nice of the neighbors to throw a welcome party for us, don't you think?"

Gretchen smiled at him. "Yes, it is. I got all the crystal and china put away in the hutch this morning. It's beginning to feel like home."

"Yeah, maybe. Tomorrow I'll finish the bookcases and we can unload our books." He retrieved a bottle of white wine from the fridge. "Come on, Gretchen, we'll be late."

They started off for Maggie and Chet's house next door, and paused on the sidewalk when a good-looking couple came toward them. "Hi, there!" the woman called. "You must be the new neighbors." Her accent sounded French. "I'm Katalie DeCarrio, and this is my husband, Gian Carlo."

Katalie was stunning, willowy and thin with long, straight blonde hair swept behind her ear on one side. Beautiful turquoise earrings dangled almost to her shoulders. She wore skinny jeans and a low-cut teal-colored blouse with a necklace that drew attention to her generous breasts. Gian Carlo smiled at Gretchen, lifted her hand to his lips, and kissed it.

Gretchen took a step backwards. "He won't bite," Katalie said quickly. "He's just Italian."

Gian Carlo was handsome, tall and lean but muscular. He had thick dark-brown hair with a bit of grey at the temples, and he wore a crisp blue shirt that brought out his steel blue eyes.

*Ah, yes. Ken and Barbie.*

They all walked into Maggie's house, and had scarcely greeted their hostess when a short, plump man bustled up to them. "Hi, I'm Tad Sabbin. You must be our new neighbors! I live a few doors down," he said, pointing behind him. "I'm a psychologist in the town of Breyer."

Jarrod and Tad shook hands and Gretchen smiled. "Nice to meet you, Tad."

"My wife, Dana, will be a little late. As usual," he added.

Gretchen caught a significant look from Maggie. *Aha. This must be part of the two-house family.* Tad had a large nose and curly grey hair; he was dressed in khakis, a Hawaiian button-down shirt, and open-toed sandals. They all walked up to Maggie's house together.

"Why don't we take that beautiful pie you brought upstairs to the kitchen," Maggie said. Gretchen followed her, admiring the beautiful walnut banister as she passed. "I had that custom-made," Maggie whispered.

The kitchen was full of chattering people, and Maggie clapped her hands. "Everybody, can I have your attention?"

All conversation stopped. "These are our new neighbors, Jarrod and Gretchen O'Malley. They moved here to be near their aging parents, and just look at this beautiful pie Gretchen made! I'm sure we'll know more about them both by the end of the evening, so everyone make yourself known to them. Oh, and one more thing. We are feasting on organically-raised pulled pork and homemade rolls that I made myself, plus a tray of vegetables and fruit fresh from my greenhouse!"

Maggie pointed to the stack of plates on the counter. "Gretchen, please be the first to help yourself."

She reached for a plate and looked at her hostess in surprise. "Your dishes are just like mine, Maggie. What a coincidence!"

Maggie shot her a smile. "I just bought them this morning."

Gretchen blinked. *Why would Maggie buy the same dishes as mine?*

The doorbell rang. "That must be Dana," Maggie said. "Gretchen, come and meet her."

Gretchen set her half-filled plate on the counter and accompanied her to the door where a heavy-set woman in her mid-sixties with curly grey hair and wearing shorts, a long-sleeved teeshirt, and flipflops stood along with three young men.

"Oh, Lucille," Maggie said in a clipped tone. "I didn't expect you tonight."

"Good thing I ran into Marie today at the grocery store," the woman grated. "She was the one who told me about this shindig tonight." She extended her hand to Gretchen. "You must be our new neighbor." She gestured behind her. "Meet my boys, Dale, Leonard, and Bruce Stanley. They're living with Larry and me temporarily until they . . . get on their feet."

Gretchen shook the woman's sweaty hand and smiled at the young men. The "boys" all looked to be in their thirties, and they were all tall and skinny with longish, unkempt hair.

"Where's Larry?" Maggie inquired in a cool voice.

"Oh, Larry can't make it tonight."

Maggie about-faced and Gretchen followed her up the stairs to find Chet. "Look who came!" Maggie announced. "Marie ran into Lucille today and told her about our party." Her voice held a distinctly sarcastic note.

At that moment Gretchen overheard Katalie say something to her husband in an undertone. "Did you lock our front door?"

Gretchen frowned, then remembered something Maggie had said about Lucille's three sons at lunch yesterday. *Ah, they must be the felons.*

Gian Carlo excused himself and left abruptly, and then Gretchen noticed an older woman standing in the doorway. She was short and stout, wearing a floral shirt, jogging pants, and sandals; her hair was grey and curly down to her shoulders. Maggie and Gretchen went to greet her.

Maggie moved forward. "Gretchen, this is Dana, Tad's wife. She lives around the corner on Little John Way. Dana is an elementary schoolteacher." Then she leaned close and whispered in her ear. "If you tell her anything, everyone in the neighborhood will know."

Gretchen extended her hand. "Nice to meet you."

"Wow," Dana said. "Everyone on the block is here!" She headed past Maggie and took the stairs up to the kitchen two at a time.

Maggie winced. "She's wearing jogging pants to my party!"

Gretchen just looked at her and smiled. *Wow. Maggie's really serious about a dress code at her parties.*

Maggie was just shutting the front door when another couple

arrived. "Hello, you two!" she said with a broad smile. "I'm glad you could make it. Gretchen, meet Marie and Darrell Levine."

Gretchen shook hands and smiled. Marie was short and thin with short, dark hair. She wore tasteful cream-colored dress slacks and a white shirt buttoned up to the collar. A pearl necklace lay just below the top button, and she had matching pearl earrings.

"It's really nice to meet you, Gretchen," Marie said in a sincere tone. "This is my husband, Darrell. He's a retired engineer. We live on the far side of the cul-de-sac. I'm a retired teacher."

Gretchen smiled. "It's very nice to meet you both."

Gretchen noted that Darrell was older, but then she took a second look at his hair. It was dyed dark brown with a purple tint! His bushy eyebrows were grey, and he had bangs that were cut straight across his forehead.

"Let's all get some dinner," Maggie said. "Marie and Darrell, the sparkling water is on the counter nearest the refrigerator."

As they went up the stairs Maggie leaned in close to Gretchen. "They're the Seventh Day Adventists I told you about," she murmured. "They don't usually come to parties where alcohol is served." Gretchen nodded.

She watched the couple enter the kitchen, where Darrell sought out Tad while Marie went to fill a plate. Lucille stood near the buffet table, sipping a glass of white wine. Gretchen drifted over to stand next to Jarrod, who was talking to Chet.

"I'm thinking about getting a new revolver for protection," Chet said. "We should go target practicing. There's a gun range down past the cornfields where acres and acres of land are used strictly for target practice."

Gretchen sighed. She didn't like guns. This would be a conversation for later, in the privacy of their own home.

One of Lucille's boys, Leonard, chimed in, his mouth full of pulled pork. "I have guns. I go to the shooting range all the time. I'm a pretty good shot."

Chet looked at him. "Did you say you have guns, Leonard?"

The boy nodded, and instantly a look of concern crossed

Chet's face.

Maggie looked at Gretchen. "I notice Dale Stanley isn't in the kitchen," she said in a quiet voice.

"Which one is Dale?" she murmured. After a moment another one of Lucille's boys emerged from the bathroom and walked past her.

"That's Dale," Maggie whispered. "He has tattoos all over his arms." She followed him into the kitchen where Chet and Jarrod were now discussing old tools.

"I have an old wooden plane," Jarrod was saying. "It belonged to my father."

"I have a lot of old tools down in the garage," Chet said.

Dale looked interested. "I'd like to see your tools."

"Maybe some other time, Dale."

"Nah, how about now?"

Chet hesitated. "Okay, why don't we all go on down to the garage."

"Oh, honey, you and your tools!" Maggie exclaimed. "Come on, Gretchen, I'll show you my craft room in the basement." Tad joined them, and they all walked downstairs together, the men heading into the garage and Gretchen and Maggie drifting into a small room where bookshelves and white baskets lined the wall. A long worktable stretched along the opposite wall, where Gretchen spied an expensive sewing machine and a wall-mounted ironing board.

"Wow," she said. "This looks really organized. What a great room for doing projects!"

Maggie just smiled and drew her on into the garage where the men were gathered. Tools hung on pegboards, and shelves along the wall were lined with labeled plastic tubs. Two bicycles hung from the ceiling. It was the most organized workshop area Gretchen had ever seen.

"Hey, Chet," Jarrod said, "this is something else! You've got everything here!"

"Yeah," Tad said. "I'm real envious of this workspace, Chet. I can't afford anything like this on my salary."

Gretchen noticed that Leonard Stanley and his brother, Dale, had joined them, but they weren't saying much. They looked at everything and ran their hands over Chet's old wooden tools.

"I'm thinking of donating these old tools to the historical society some day," Chet said.

"Huh?" Dale said. "Why do that when you can sell these things for a lot of money?"

The men stared at him in silence until Maggie spoke up. "Let's all go back to the party." She sent Chet a look. "Honey," she whispered, "be sure you lock the garage door." Maggie did not look happy.

"Is anything wrong?" Gretchen asked.

"Oh, no. No, nothing's wrong. It's just that I can't find the key to my crystal cupboard."

Chet's head swiveled around. "I left it in the lock this morning, Maggie."

"Well, it's not there now," she whispered.

"Wait a minute," her husband said under his breath. "Where's Bruce?

"Wasn't he with you down in the garage?" They looked at each other for a long moment without speaking. After a long minute Maggie returned to the kitchen and Chet began replenishing drinks for the guests.

Gretchen sipped her gin and tonic and found herself listening to the conversations swirling around her. She learned that Gian Carlo was an attorney, like Jarrod. "I used to be a DC lawyer," he confided, "but Katalie and I had no time for each other."

Jarrod nodded. "I know what you mean. I help set up businesses, and that sort of career kinda eats you up."

"What line of business is Chet in?" Jarrod asked.

"No one knows what he does," Gian Carlo said quickly. "But they seem very well off." Then he added something odd. "Maggie has the worst luck. She's always hurting herself. She spent all last year in a wheelchair, and we still don't know exactly why."

The women gathered at one end of the kitchen, discussing careers. When Gretchen confessed she used to be a preschool teacher, the other women looked interested. "Well," Dana said, "at least you had a job."

Gretchen had no idea what she meant by her comment since Dana herself was an elementary schoolteacher.

"I'm so lucky to be a stay-at-home mom," Maggie said.

Dana's eyebrows went up. "Does that mean Chet is a stay-at-home father?"

The other women stared at Dana, and Gretchen moved away to stand next to Katalie. When she got the chance she leaned over and voiced something she'd been wondering about. "What is with Lucille and her boys?" she said in a low tone.

The young Frenchwoman leaned in close. "I'll tell you another time," she murmured.

At that moment, Maggie walked over. "What are you two whispering about, my cooking?"

Gretchen smiled at her. "The buffet is delicious, Maggie. And your home is really beautiful. It was really nice of you to bring the neighborhood together like this."

"My pleasure, Gretchen. No trouble at all."

"I'll stay and help you clean up if you like."

"Don't be silly, there's no need. My maid will come

tomorrow."

When the party wound down, Gretchen sought out Maggie in the kitchen where she was making up doggie bags of pulled pork and rolls for the guests. "Thank you again, Maggie."

"Of course." Maggie grinned at her. "You needed a proper welcome to our neighborhood."

Gretchen and Jarrod were the last to leave. They were about to head for the front door when suddenly Maggie said something to Chet that surprised her. "Can you believe that Lucille brought the boys tonight?"

"Yeah, really hard to figure," he said. "Better take a good look around the house to see if anything is missing."

Gretchen gasped. "What?"

"Wait a minute," Jarrod said. "Do we have to worry about those boys?"

"Well ..." Chet hesitated. "You might as well know. At least two of them have criminal records."

"Oh, my lord," Gretchen murmured. By the time she and Jarrod returned to their own house, she had worked up a healthy suspicion of Lucille's "boys." Later, when she thought over events at the party, she suddenly remembered that she hadn't seen one of the boys, Bruce, for most of the evening. Maybe Maggie wasn't exaggerating when she described them as criminals.

"Jarrod, be sure you lock all our doors and windows tonight."

He sent her an odd look. "Any special reason?"

"N-no. I'm just feeling uneasy."

Chapter Five

# The More the Merrier

Gretchen stood over the heating vent in her kitchen, rubbing her hands together. "The weather has sure turned cold overnight!" she said to herself. Her red plaid wool scarf was still draped over the kitchen chair from her outing the day before, so she wrapped it around her neck for extra warmth and picked up her coffee mug. She had just taken a sip when she glanced out the back window.

A woman was visible in the window of the house behind her. She thought about waving, but something stopped her, and then she saw what it was. The woman was peering at her window using binoculars! Wow, that was really weird. *Is she looking right into my kitchen?*

"Jarrod?"

No answer.

She walked into the living room to find her husband sitting in his leather recliner, reading the financial section of the New York Times.

"Hey, you!" she said with a smile.

Jarrod looked up and set the newspaper aside. "What's up?"

"You know that woman who lives in the house behind us? I just caught her looking at me through the window with binoculars!"

He grinned. "Did you wave at her?"

"I don't think it's funny, Jarrod. And no, I did not wave at her."

He went back to reading his newspaper. She waited for him to say something more, but he was absorbed in the Times. Finally she shrugged and turned to leave.

"I'm going to the grocery store to order the turkey for Thanksgiving."

"Um-hmmm." He didn't look up, even when she pulled her keys out of her jeans. When Jarrod was reading anything he gave it his full attention, and that was a trait she loved to hate about him. Her husband could tune out and turn things off with a switch.

Gretchen couldn't tune anything out. Her mind was always swirling with all the things that needed to be done, and when they needed to be finished, and what the next step was. Thanksgiving was two weeks away and her thoughts were already stuffed full of plans. And worries. She always worried about things coming up, and today was no different. She wasn't even completely unpacked yet, and this would be their first dinner for the family in their new home. She was feeling a little bit anxious.

She drove down Robin Hood Boulevard, noticing that the trees had lost all their leaves and the streets were wet and dark-looking. Dirty snow was starting to pile up near the curbs. Everything looked cold and wintry, so she decided to stop at Strudel Bakery for a quick cup of coffee and mull over her to-do list for Thanksgiving. She pulled the Lexus into the parking lot, wrapped her plaid wool scarf around her neck, and climbed out of the car.

The bakery was right out of the fifties, with a grey countertop and pink and grey vinyl swivel chairs. The walls were painted light pink and grey and covered with old photographs of bakers in aprons and puffy white chef's caps and kids drinking sodas with two straws. She recognized "Earth Angel" playing on a jukebox against one wall.

She ordered coffee and had just turned away from the cash register when she spied Maggie sitting alone in the far corner, crying.

"Maggie? Are you all right?"

Maggie stiffened and turned her face away. "Oh, Gretchen. I didn't expect to see you here." When she turned back, Maggie was dabbing at her eyes with a paper napkin.

"What's wrong?"

"N-nothing." She sniffled and swiped her fingers across her cheeks. "I'm fine, really."

Gretchen sat down across from her. "Maggie, you are obviously not fine. What is it?"

Maggie sent her a wobbly smile. "Oh, I guess it's nothing

life-shattering. My family just decided they're not coming for Thanksgiving after all."

"Oh. That's too bad. You must be disappointed." Gretchen took a sip of her coffee and waited.

"This will be our first holiday without any of Chet's or my family. The kids have decided to go to their in-laws for Thanksgiving, and . . . and we weren't invited." Her voice trailed off and she pressed the napkin against her eyes.

"That must be hard," Gretchen said. "I'm really sorry."

Maggie nodded. "My kids' in-laws are really dysfunctional human beings, but I'm still going to miss being there. Does that make any sense?" She blotted tears off her cheeks.

Gretchen reached over and patted her hand. "You don't need to be alone on Thanksgiving."

Maggie looked up. "What do you mean?"

"You and Chet can come to our house for Thanksgiving! You can meet our family and enjoy turkey and all the trimmings with us."

"Oh, my. Gretchen, are you serious? We wouldn't be

imposing?"

"Of course not. The more the merrier. It will be fun!" She stood up. "I was just on my way to the grocery store, so I've got to get go— "

Maggie shot to her feet and hugged her. "I can go shopping with you!" she said, her voice eager. "I know exactly what we need to get for Thanksgiving dinner."

"Oh, no, Maggie. I can do my own grocery shopping. You and Chet just show up at our house on Thanksgiving day."

"Don't forget to get a Willy Bird turkey at the A & P on the other end of town," Maggie said. "They have the best turkeys. I'll come over early and help stuff the bird and make sure we stay on task."

Gretchen raised her eyebrows. "Oh, no. You and Chet come over an hour or two before I serve dinner. And I'm ordering my turkey from Val's, next door to the bookstore."

"Oh. Well, I could come to the store with you. You know, make sure you pick out the best turkey."

Gretchen tried to keep smiling. "Don't be silly, Maggie. I've made Thanksgiving dinners for years."

"Well, of course you have, Gretchen. But I'll still come over and help you make dinner. That's half the fun of Thanksgiving!"

She drew in a long, slow breath. "Maggie," she said firmly. "Jarrod and I have this covered. I want you and Chet to come later in the day, as I said before. Now, I'm afraid I need to run some errands."

"But we have to make out the menu for dinner," Maggie said.

"Never you mind about the menu. You and Chet are our guests for Thanksgiving."

"Oh."

"Now, I really have to go." She walked out the door and headed for the parking lot.

In her car, she sat still for a moment to collect her thoughts. *Wow, it sounds like Maggie wants to supervise my cooking!*

She walked slowly across the parking lot toward Val's supermarket. People were bustling everywhere, mothers pushing strollers, kids on skateboards, a group of teenaged girls all talking on their cell phones and paying no attention to each other.

The store windows were decorated with holiday displays, and one in particular caught her eye. Blumme Florist. She walked in and admired the beautiful antique dark maple table covered with a cream-colored lace tablecloth. It was set with gold charger plates, red napkins, and gold-rimmed stemware, and the centerpiece was a sparkly gold platter nestled on a bed of evergreens.

Oh, a centerpiece like that would be perfect for Thanksgiving! She was looking for the price tag when a short woman wearing a red apron and a smile appeared.

"Hello, can I help you?"

Gretchen looked up. "I'm interested in that beautiful arrangement in your front window, the one on the table."

The woman's smile widened. "Would you like one sent to someone out of town?"

"Actually, I would like one for my own Thanksgiving table."

The florist pulled a pen and notepad from her apron pocket,

and Gretchen gave her the street address.

"Oh, you live next door to the Gaineses?"

"Why, yes, I do."

The woman looked Gretchen up and down, then went back to her notepad. "Maggie said you were short."

*What? My goodness, people in this town sure talk a lot. And everyone seems to talk to Maggie.*

"I'll deliver your arrangement the eighteenth, around noon, if that's all right. By the way, I'm Annie Blumme. I own this shop."

"Hello, Annie." Gretchen smiled at her.

"I heard new neighbors had moved in from Lafayette last month." She leaned toward Gretchen and lowered her voice. "Maggie told me all about you and your husband."

"Oh?"

"She thinks you're great! Not like those other nosy neighbors you have."

Gretchen caught her breath. *What 'nosy neighbors'?* She wanted to ask who they were, but then she'd be acting like a nosy neighbor herself.

*I wonder what else Maggie has spread around about Jarrod and me?*

A bit unnerved, she left the florist and walked next door to the Shellville Bookstore. Gretchen peered at the display of books in the front window, then on impulse she walked in.

A bookish-looking young woman sat behind the cash register. "May I help you?"

"I'm just looking around your store. I've never been in before."

"Are you new in town? Or just traveling through?"

"I'm new. I've just moved from Lafayette."

The clerk pushed her glasses up off her forehead. "Oh, you must be Maggie's new neighbor!"

*Holy cow! Did Maggie publish a newsletter about us the day we moved in?*

"Maggie's told me all about you and your husband. She said you sure had a lot of boxes to unpack!"

Gretchen blinked. *What else is Maggie telling everyone*

*about us? I'd better start watching what I say to her.*

The clerk extended her hand across the counter. "I'm Sandra Livingston, Mrs. O'Malley. Let me know if I can help you find anything."

Gretchen wandered around from the art and architecture section to the fiction section and finally selected a novel, "The Help." At the cash register she slipped her credit card from her wallet.

"That is a great book," Sandra gushed. "And the movie is wonderful, too. Have you seen it?"

"No. I've been busy unpacking all those boxes Maggie told you about."

"I love to read personal stories about people," Sandra said as she slipped the book into a Shellville Bookstore bag. "I'm also writing a memoir."

Gretchen studied the bookstore owner's thin face. "Really?"

"Oh, yes. I've been working on it for years. It's about our town, Shellville, and the people who live here. Maybe one day I'll publish it."

"That sounds very interesting," Gretchen said with a polite smile.

Sandra laughed. "If I ever do publish my book I'll have to move away. All the town secrets, you know."

Gretchen picked up her purchase and moved toward the door. "It was nice to meet you, Sandra."

"Likewise," Sandra called. "I'll tell Maggie I met her new neighbor!"

Gretchen's last stop was Val's market at the end of the mall. Once inside she walked to the back where the meat department was and rang the bell on the countertop. A tall, thin man with a grey beard and a stained white apron approached.

"I'd like to order a turkey for Thanksgiving."

He poised his pencil over a pad of paper. "Name?"

"Gretchen O'Malley."

"Ah. You're Maggie's new neighbor. I know all about you."

Gretchen stared at him.

"Maggie was in just a few minutes ago. She's already put your name on the list for turkeys."

She looked at him in disbelief. "I beg your pardon?"

"Yeah, let's see." He thumbed back through his pad. "Yep, she ordered a twenty-four-pound Butterball turkey for you."

"Did she now?" Gretchen folded her arms across her midriff. "But I only want a twenty-pound turkey."

"Sorry. We're sold out of the twenty-pounders, so Maggie thought it would be safer to get a bigger one since she and Chet are joining you and your family for Thanksgiving dinner."

Gretchen gritted her teeth. "Oh? And what else did Maggie say?"

He didn't even blink. "She said that you really should be getting a Willie Bird instead of a Butterball turkey."

"Really," she said, her tone flat. "What I want is a twenty-four-pound Butterball turkey. And I'd like two pounds of fresh crab and two pounds of large prawns."

He shook his head but wrote it down. "Maggie was hoping you were also having a ham," he said. "Specifically, a Spiral Ham." He raised his eyebrows and waited expectantly.

"Not this year," she said decisively. "I will pick up the

turkey and the fish the day before Thanksgiving."

"Uh . . . won't work," the butcher said. "Maggie wants to soak the turkey in brine for two days before you roast it."

"Oh, she does, does she? Is there anything else that Maggie wants?" She couldn't help spitting the words out.

"Well, it's none of my business, but you're lucky Maggie's coming. She's an awesome chef. She's taken cooking classes all over the world."

Gretchen looked the butcher in the eye. "Then this will be a treat for her, not having to do any cooking this year, won't it?"

By the time she reached the end of Robin Hood Boulevard she had calmed down, but when she passed Little John Way she noticed a woman with a clipboard sitting in a lawn chair under the open door of her garage. She was older, wearing grey sweatpants and boots, and a fuzzy scarf was wound around her head. Gretchen slowed down, and the woman glanced up and smiled at her, and then waved.

*That's weird. I wonder what she's doing?* She took a last look in the rear view mirror and noticed that binoculars hung around the woman's neck.

*That's the woman who was peering into my kitchen window this morning!*

She pulled into her driveway and flew up the stairs. "Jarrod, I'm home! I just saw that woman with the binoculars again!"

"Honey," he yelled, "Chet's here."

She stopped short at the kitchen door and gaped at the sight. Chet and Jarrod were bent over a greasy motor of some kind sitting in the middle of her kitchen table. Oil had soaked into the tablecloth and was dripping onto the floor.

"Jarrod, what is that thing?"

He straightened. "It's a lawnmower motor," he said apologetically. "Chet brought it over and— "

"In my kitchen? Why is it in my kitchen?"

Chet gave her a weak smile. "Maggie wouldn't let me work on it at our house."

"And that makes it okay to use *my house*? My *kitchen*?"

"Well ... it's really cold in the garage, and Jarrod said it would be okay."

Jarrod shook his head. "No, I merely said— "

"Get it out of my kitchen!" She spun away and started down the hall. Jarrod followed her.

"Honey," he whispered.

"Don't 'honey' me, Jarrod! Look at your hands, they're all greasy. Don't touch anything!"

"Honey, listen. Chet just showed up and barged into the house with that thing all wrapped up. I've been trying to get rid of him. Boy, that man can be really pushy."

"Out!" she ordered.

"Okay, okay." He turned back toward the kitchen, but she stopped him.

"Maggie is pushy, too."

"Yeah? They sure make a pair, don't they?" He started back down the hall, and she cleared her throat.

"I don't know how to tell you this, Jarrod, but I invited Maggie and Chet to Thanksgiving dinner."

He stopped dead. "You what?"

"I ran into Maggie at the bakery. She was crying because her

*Erina Bridget Ring*

kids aren't coming for Thanksgiving, and I felt so sorry for her I invited her to our house. It just popped out of my mouth."

Jarrod rolled his eyes and groaned. "Oh, man, did you really invite them?"

Gretchen sighed. "Maybe it will be all right. As long as Chet doesn't bring another greasy motor along, what could go wrong?"

Chapter Six

## Guess Who's Coming to Dinner?

The week before Thanksgiving Gretchen had her appointment with her new doctor. She arrived at his office 30 minutes early, and when she walked up to the counter she froze. Her neighbor, Dorothy, was sitting behind the reception desk, her head down, talking on the phone. Gretchen took a deep breath.

"Oh, Gretchen," Dorothy said as she hung up the phone. "Hello."

"Hi, Dorothy."

"What are you doing here today?"

"I have an appointment. I'm a new patient."

Dorothy thumbed through the stack of paperwork on her desk. "I have the new patient paperwork right here."

Gretchen filled it all out and handed it back, then watched Dorothy turn the pages and read them with interest. She wanted to grab it out of her hands, but it was too late. She'd listed everything, all her personal information, everything. Should a receptionist be reading this? She thought only physicians and their assistants were privy to private patient information.

When her name was called, Dorothy announced loudly, "This is my new neighbor!"

Wishing she was invisible, she edged past the receptionist's desk and followed the nurse down the hall, donned a hospital gown, and waited until she heard a tap on the door.

But it wasn't the doctor who stepped in, it was Dorothy!

"Golly, Gretchen, I'm surprised to see you here," Dorothy said. "You look perfectly normal to me."

*What? What business is it of hers? What's she doing here, anyway?*

She opened her mouth to say something, but at that moment Dr. Ruggiero walked in. He was an older man, tall and thin, with grey hair and glasses. After an hour's conversation, the doctor renewed her prescription for blood pressure medication, and she dressed and walked to the front desk to make a follow-up appointment.

Dorothy asked to see the prescription. "I want to photocopy it," she said.

Maggie's warning popped into her mind and she hesitated. *Don't tell Dorothy anything because it will be spread all over the neighborhood.*

"I said," Dorothy repeated, "give me your prescription so I can copy it."

Gretchen sucked in her breath and looked right at her. "Dorothy, this is a private matter between me and my doctor."

"Why, Gretchen, I am appalled you would say that. Of course it's private. Sharing such information would be a breach of patient confidentiality."

Gretchen sent her a long look and handed her the prescription.

\*     \*     \*

On Thanksgiving day Gretchen woke early to the sound of the wind whistling through the bare tree limbs outside. She sat up and peered between the slat of the window blinds. *Oh, good heavens, another foot of snow has fallen.*

"It's going to be another snowy day," she said to Jarrod. "I hope the kids won't have a problem getting here."

Jarrod rolled over. "Um-hmmm."

"I'm going to set the table and start the turkey stuffing. You just stay in bed and catch up on your sleep." She tried to keep the sarcasm out of her voice. She was tying her pink robe in front when she heard his sleepy voice."

"Honey?"

She turned in the doorway. "Yes?"

"When do the kids get here?"

"They're picking up Mom and Dad so they should be here by 4 o'clock."

"Okay."

"Jarrod? Do you want to make the stuffing? I'll baste the turkey when you're finished."

"Sure," he said. "I'll get up in a few minutes and do it. The kids love my stuffing."

In the kitchen Gretchen poured herself a cup of coffee and

opened the window blinds. New snow covered everything. She was gazing at the sparkling scene for a long minute, sipping her coffee, when suddenly she got the feeling she wasn't alone. She narrowed her eyes and studied the back yard and the house behind theirs.

*What on earth ... ?* There was the woman she'd seen yesterday, the one with the clipboard, standing at *her* window, peering at her through binoculars. Why was that woman always looking out her window?

She decided to wave. "Happy Thanksgiving," she mouthed. Then she decided she had no time for this today. She had to arrange the dining room table and chop up onions and celery for Jarrod to use in the stuffing and do a hundred other things to get ready for Thanksgiving dinner.

She turned away from the window and opened the silverware drawer as a yawning Jarrod appeared in the doorway, still in his pajamas.

"Morning, honey!"

"There's coffee on the table for you," she said.

He took his coffee over to the window and looked out. "Looks like a snowy winter ahead." He started to drink from the mug in his hand and suddenly jerked, spilling the liquid down his pajama top. "Gretchen, there's a woman waving at me from her window!"

"Yes, I know. She's been there at her window, watching us, since the first day we moved in. Just wave back at her."

He shot her a look, gave a half-hearted wave, and ducked back out of sight. Gretchen laughed.

"It doesn't matter where you stand, Jarrod. She has binoculars so she can still see you."

"Well, then," he said with a grin. "Let's give her something to talk about." He walked up behind her at the silverware drawer, turned her around and bent her backwards in a passionate kiss.

"Jarrod, stop!" she gasped.

"Nope," he whispered in her ear. "I bet she's writing this down on her clipboard."

They straightened, laughing like teenagers, and looked out the window. "You're right," she said. "She's writing something."

The doorbell rang.

"Good God," Jarrod blurted, "it's only eight o'clock! Who would that be at this hour?"

"I bet you a hundred dollars it's Maggie."

"At eight in the morning?"·

Gretchen sighed. "I told her to come this afternoon, with Chet. Not this morning. Or maybe it's a delivery man." She walked down to the front door and peeked through the security lens. Good Lord, it *was* Maggie. And she was all dressed up for dinner!

Gretchen took a deep breath and opened the door a crack. "Maggie, I'm still in my robe. We're just having our morning coffee."

Maggie looked unruffled. "Don't you ever get dressed at a reasonable hour?"

Gretchen stared at her. *How rude!*

"No one tells me what to do in my own house," she said firmly. "Some of us like to take our time in the morning."

"Well, I guess so," Maggie replied. "What do you want me

to do, go home?" She rubbed her hands together for warmth.

"Well, yes, as a matter of fact. I invited you to come this afternoon."

Maggie sighed. "Oh, all right. But call me if you need me."

"Oh, I will," Gretchen said sweetly. "She closed the door with a decisive clunk.

"Who was that?" Jarrod asked.

"Maggie. Dressed up in wool slacks and a beautiful red turtleneck with a floral scarf and jewelry everywhere. She looks really put together, and at this hour of the morning."

"Yeah, really makes you wonder," Jarrod said. "Maybe she never goes to bed."

Gretchen bit her lip. "Maybe I should get dressed up for dinner, too."

"Not me, honey. It's my day off and I'm watching some football."

"You do remember we're having company for Thanksgiving dinner," she reminded.

"So? I hope they like me in jeans and a tee-shirt!" he said

with a laugh as he opened the refrigerator. "Where are the onions and the celery?"

\*     \*     \*

An hour later the phone rang, and when Gretchen hung up she was shaking. "It's Dad. He's short of breath, and Justine and Darren are taking him to Emergency."

They dressed quickly, climbed into Jarrod's black BMW, and discovered the garage door wouldn't open because of piled-up snow. Jarrod got out the snow blower he kept in the garage while Gretchen wrung her hands and tried to keep calm. In five minutes there was enough snow cleared to back the car out.

They made a left turn on Robin Hood Boulevard, and when they passed Little John Way, there was the binocular woman sitting in a folding chair under her open garage door. She had on a furry hat and she held a clipboard in her hand. She waved at them as they went by.

Jarrod frowned. "That's the same woman who was watching us through the window," he said.

"Yes," Gretchen sighed. Just then her cell phone rang.

It was Maggie. "I heard you left your house in a hurry," she said. "Anything wrong? Are we still on for dinner this afternoon?"

"Oh, Maggie, my father is on his way to the hospital."

"Gee, that's too bad, Gretchen."

"Wait a minute. How did you know we'd left the house?"

"Oh," Maggie said quickly, "you know how news travels."

"No, I don't," Gretchen said. "Enlighten me."

"Well . . ." Maggie seemed to hunt for words. "I saw Jarrod snow-blowing your driveway and then you drove off really fast. So I . . . Will you be back in time for dinner?"

Gretchen blinked. "Dinner? Oh, yes, Thanksgiving. Maggie, I really don't know, but I'll let you know, all right?"

"Now don't you worry about it," Maggie said soothingly. "You just take care of your father. And be sure to call me with updates."

Gretchen looked over at Jarrod. "It looks like there's more than one woman watching us."

At Mercy Hospital they waited hours while tests were run,

and finally Gretchen's father was sent home with a warning about letting himself get dehydrated. They met with the caregiver, settled him in at Justine's house, and drove home in silence.

"It's getting dark and another snowstorm is predicted," Jarrod said after awhile.

Gretchen took a deep breath. "I know. Not soon enough to keep Maggie and Chet at home, though."

By the time they reached Shellville it was after seven. They drove down Robin Hood Boulevard and suddenly Jarrod stopped the car. Flashing red lights were blinking at the end of their block. "I wonder what's going on?"

Two fire trucks, three police cars, and an ambulance were parked in front of their house. Jarrod stopped the car a block away and they ran for their front door.

It stood wide open. They raced up the stairs to the kitchen, which seemed to be in complete chaos. "What is going on here?" Jarrod yelled.

"Throw it out on the porch," someone shouted.

"Throw what out?" he demanded. "What's happening?"

"It smells like something burning," Gretchen said. "I didn't leave anything cooking when we left."

A fireman in full gear walked over. "Is this your house?"

"Yes," Jarrod replied.

"You're real lucky this woman called us when she saw the microwave had caught on fire." He pointed to someone on the deck outside the kitchen. "By the time we got here she'd unplugged it from the wall. She was real smart not to open the microwave door."

"Microwave!" Gretchen exclaimed. "I didn't leave anything in the microwave."

The fireman nodded. "We tossed it off the back porch into the snow, but by that time the fire had gone out by itself. Lots of smoke, though. Doesn't look like there's any damage other than the smell."

"Oh," Gretchen said in a small voice.

"The potatoes didn't make it, though."

"What potatoes?" she asked. "We weren't home, so how—

?"

The fireman gestured toward the back deck. And then Maggie walked out of the shadows and into the house. She was wearing what she'd had on that morning, and high stiletto heels, of all things.

Gretchen gaped at her. "Maggie? What in the world are you doing here?"

Maggie wrapped her arms across her waist. "Well, I . . . I knew you weren't going to be home in time to cook Thanksgiving dinner, so I came over to do it for you! I put a few potatoes in the microwave to bake and . . ." Her voice trailed off. "Well, they caught on fire. I don't usually use a microwave, and I guess I put them in for too long."

"How did you get into our house?"

Maggie pointed to the sliding door onto the deck. "You left the back door unlocked."

Jarrod shot Gretchen a look. "You came over to cook dinner in our house while we were gone?"

"We wanted to surprise you," Maggie explained. "I told you

we were a close-knit neighborhood."

"We?" Gretchen and Jarrod said in one voice. "Who is 'we'?"

Maggie tipped her head toward the back deck. There stood a group of their neighbors in the snow. "I'm sorry, Gretchen," she said. "We'll buy you a new microwave."

Gretchen just looked at her, and then at Jarrod.

"The turkey is almost finished," Maggie said, "and I set the table and put the salads and the pies on the side-hutch. I also set up an extra table for the neighbors."

Gretchen couldn't believe what she was hearing.

But Maggie wasn't finished. "I also called your daughter and son-in-law, Justine and Darren, is it? Anyway, I invited them to come back into town for Thanksgiving dinner tonight."

"You what? How did you get their phone numbers?"

Maggie pointed to the police officer on the staircase. He cleared his throat. "Mrs. Gaines said there was a medical emergency."

"I didn't see the harm in it," Maggie cried. "In an

emergency, well, you know, the police can . . . you know."

The fireman waved an arm at Gretchen's kitchen. "Looks like you're real lucky it was just the microwave and not an oven fire. Usually on Thanksgiving we get calls for burning turkeys and clogged fireplaces."

Gretchen just nodded. "I didn't know that," she said tightly.

Maggie clutched her arm. "And look who showed up for dinner!"

"Who?" she asked. She wasn't at all sure she wanted to know.

"She's in the dining room."

Gretchen looked. At the far end of the table was the binocular woman. She had on her furry hat, and the binoculars still hung from a strap around her neck. Her clipboard lay on the table beside her.

Maggie beamed and gestured toward her. "You remember Gladys. She was the one who called to tell me you'd left your house in a rush."

Gladys smiled and lifted one hand to wave. Gretchen

decided not to wave back.

*     *     *

Late that night, when the windows were finally closed, the smell of smoke and burning potatoes had dissipated, and the house had heated up again, Gretchen and Jarrod sat side by side on the sofa, shaking their heads in disbelief. "Whoever would have thought we had neighbors who would break into our house on Thanksgiving to cook dinner?" Gretchen mused.

"And start a fire in our kitchen, call the fire department, get the police to give them an unlisted family phone number, and then— "

"Invite over the woman who spies on us," Gretchen finished.

"And," Jarrod added, "pretend that nothing bad happened." He took her hand. "Gretchen, honey, I know I locked the sliding door to the back deck before we left. I always check it."

"I know you do, Jarrod."

"So, don't you have to wonder how they really got into our house?"

Chapter Seven

# Holiday Surprise

It took days of airing out the house before the burnt potato smell was gone. Just in time, too. Christmas was right around the corner.

Gretchen spent the morning wrestling four boxes of Christmas ornaments down from the attic, then set up the seven-foot pre-lit tree dead center in the living room window and began to unpack the boxes. She carefully hung the ornaments on the branches, positioning each sentimental one in just the right spot, then kicked off her slippers and stood on tiptoe to attach the star on the top.

She looked up and spied the mail truck making its way around the neighborhood cul-de- sac. It stopped at the curb and Gretchen raced out into the snow for the mail. Too late she realized she was barefoot.

The driver smiled. "I'm Betty. You must be the new neighbors!"

"Yes, we are." She jogged in place to keep her feet from freezing.

Betty handed her a stack of envelopes. The one on top had holly leaves around the border and bold hand-lettering. Gretchen thanked Betty and dashed back inside where she took the holly-leaf letter out of the pile of bills and walked over to stand over the heating vent to warm her icy feet.

"Oh, it's an invitation!"

*The Neighborhood*

## *Annual Christmas Progressive Dinner*

### *Sunday, December 17th*

*Appetizers*      **Katalie and Gian Carlo DeCarrio**

*Dinner*      **Marie and Darrell Levine**

*Dessert*      **Reilly and Dorothy Hogan**

*Bring a dish to share – Holiday dress – RSVP*

Gretchen pinned the invitation to the refrigerator door and had just gone back to decorating the Christmas tree when Jarrod appeared in the doorway.

"Hi, honey. Guess what? We're invited to a progressive dinner on the seventeenth."

"I hope no one microwaves any potatoes!" he quipped.

She couldn't help laughing. "Dinner is at Marie and Darrell Levine's. Let's hope they aren't fans of baked potatoes." She went upstairs to call Katalie and volunteer to bring wine. When she hung up the phone something outside the bedroom window caught her attention. My goodness, there was Gladys, standing in the snow in the middle of her back yard, looking at something through her binoculars. The woman glanced up, saw Gretchen, grinned, and gave her a thumbs up.

Gretchen smiled and waved, then walked into the living room to switch on the Christmas tree lights and put Nat King Cole on the CD player. Snow was falling. The sun was just setting, and she sat down to admire the tree. *It's beginning to look a lot like Christmas . . .*

Jarrod sat down beside her. "I love this time of year," he said.

"I do, too. It's so peaceful and happy."

"Let's go to Maria's Kitchen for dinner." When she agreed, he unplugged the tree lights and double-checked the sliding door onto the deck. "No more potatoes," he murmured. Gretchen laughed.

When he backed the Lexus out of the garage, she noticed that every single house in the neighborhood had put up lights and arranged decorations on their lawns. "Wow! Our neighbors have been busy today. Look at Reilly and Dorothy's house!"

Images of deer were scattered all over their front lawn. Blue and green lights played over the front yard to simulate water, from which the animals were drinking. Behind the deer a wooden manger was lit up, with a life-sized Mary and Joseph and the Three Wise Men looking over the Baby Jesus.

"Jarrod, look!"

"I see it," he said dryly.

"No, I mean behind the Wise Men. See that turkey? It's outlined in lights."

"What turkey? What's a turkey got to do with Christmas?"

Gretchen sighed. "Beats me. It's pretty colorful, though."

"I am not decorating like that," Jarrod announced. "This year we'll be lucky to get a strand of lights on the house."

Maggie and Chet's house had a snowman in the yard and seven of Santa's elves riding bicycles next to it. "That's cute, but a bit much," Gretchen murmured. "Jarrod, slow down. I hear something." She rolled her window down. Sure enough, "Joy to the World" floated out of the elves' toy shop set up near the front door.

"Listen!"

"Holy cow. These people sure like to decorate for Christmas."

But the best was yet to come. As they passed Little John Way, there was Gladys waving at them from her folding chair which was outlined with Christmas lights. Even her clipboard was lit up. Around her neck she wore a necklace of flashing mini-lights, and at her feet sat a portable heater with a big red bow on top.

They laughed all the way to the restaurant.

\*     \*     \*

The following day when Jarrod left to meet with a client, Gretchen peeked through the living room blinds and saw Dorothy Hogan from next door coming up the sidewalk. "I wonder where she's going so early? And she's still in her bathrobe!"

The doorbell rang. "Dorothy! I'm not dressed yet." *Don't the neighbors around here ever bother to call before they visit?*

"I'm not dressed, either," the tall, heavy-set woman said. "But I really need to talk to someone."

"Oh. Well, come on in. I'm just making coffee."

Dorothy walked over to the kitchen window. "I see Gladys has a good view of your house, too."

Gretchen looked out to see Gladys waving. "What's up, Dorothy?" She poured two mugs of coffee and motioned her to sit down at the kitchen table.

"Well," she huffed. "Reilly has really done it this time."

"Done what?"

"He's a hunter. Did you know that?"

"No, I didn't."

Dorothy sighed and took a sip of her coffee. "My husband is addicted to killing anything he gets in his gun sights. And after he shoots it, he stuffs it! He stuffs everything." She burst into tears.

Gretchen was at a loss. "Lots of men like to hunt," she said at last. "What exactly is the problem?"

Dorothy snuffled back tears. "The problem? The problem is

that today he told me what my Christmas present is this year."

"Oh? What is it?"

"It's a . . . Oh, my God, Gretchen. It's a stuffed turkey! A turkey with its wings fanned open behind it." She blew her nose.

Gretchen thought that was the funniest thing she'd heard in a long time. She put her fingers over her mouth to stifle a laugh and focused on the view out her kitchen window.

"A stuffed turkey," Dorothy continued in an injured tone. "A *male* turkey."

Her face looked blotchy. "Reilly says it's the biggest turkey he'd ever seen. The glass display case alone will be as big as my sofa."

Gretchen gasped. *Oh, this poor woman.*

"What do I do?" Dorothy asked in a serious voice.

Gretchen bit the inside of her cheek. "Oh, Dorothy I don't know. Maybe you could . . . ah . . . tell Reilly you would . . . um . . . rather have a nice pair of earrings for Christmas?"

"Gretchen, it's not a joke."

"Of course not. Truly I can see what a serious matter it is."

Dorothy moaned. "There is absolutely no place in my house to put a damned stuffed turkey in a damn glass case!"

"Maybe you could suggest he put it in the garage somewhere?"

"Don't I wish! You don't understand these hunters, Gretchen. They're absolutely obsessed with their trophies. They spend hours talking about a hunting trip and more hours getting ready for it, and after it's all over and they've slaughtered some poor innocent animal, they spend hours looking at the pictures they took of it."

Gretchen stared at her.

"Whatever you do, Gretchen, don't let Jarrod get sucked into any hunting trip with the men on this block."

"Jarrod doesn't hunt," she said with relief.

"He will if Reilly gets hold of him."

"Oh, I don't think so. I know Jarrod pretty well."

"And another thing," Dorothy continued. "Someone always gets hurt when they go hunting with Reilly."

An alarm went off in Gretchen's brain. "Hurt? How do they

get hurt?"

"Reilly accidentally shoots them."

"What?"

"Then he blames the guy for not listening to him." She started to cry again. "I hate hunting season!"

Thank God at that moment the doorbell rang. Gretchen patted Dorothy's shoulder and escaped to answer the door.

"Maggie!" She opened the door. "Maggie, I'm still in my bathrobe."

"So am I," Maggie chirped. "I saw Dorothy come over in *her* robe, so I got undressed and put on my pajamas and decided to come over and visit, too."

"You got back into your pajamas to come . . . ?" Gretchen's voice failed.

Maggie beamed at her. "Well, yes, I did. Since you don't seem to get dressed early in the day, I decided to try it myself."

*Oh, my gosh, what is this woman thinking?*

"Dorothy came to see me," she said pointedly. "We are having a private talk."

"Oh, I can be discreet." Maggie brushed past her into the kitchen. "Hi, Dorothy!"

Gretchen stared at her. *Those are her 'pajamas'? A red satin negligee and high-heeled slippers of red fur?*

"Oh, Maggie," Dorothy said, her tone flat. "Hello." The kitchen went suddenly quiet. Gretchen frowned at the chill in the air. Apparently Dorothy and Maggie were not friendly. How awkward.

"How about a quick cup of coffee?" she said in desperation. "Then I— I have a ton of things to do today."

"Oh?" Maggie's eyes snapped with curiosity. "Where are you going?"

"Um . . . just doing errands."

"I have errands today, too," Maggie said with a smile.

"*Personal* errands." She hoped Maggie would take the hint.

Dorothy stood up, her face still looking blotchy. "Gretchen, could you walk me out the door?"

In the doorway, Dorothy leaned in close. "Don't tell Maggie anything. I mean it, Gretchen. Not a word! Remember, I know something about you." She gripped Gretchen's hand and fled.

*What on earth is going on? Was that a threat?*

A chill went down her spine.

Back in her kitchen, she scooped the coffee mugs off the table and set them in the sink. "Maggie, I'm sorry, but I have to run. I have . . . an appointment. But thanks for stopping by."

Maggie's eyes dimmed. "Oh. Oh, well, I should be going."

Gretchen watched her turn toward the stairway. "Do be careful going down the steps in those lovely fur slippers." She was never this catty, but Maggie really punched one of her buttons.

Late that afternoon when Jarrod came home she told him about Dorothy coming over in her bathrobe, and the stuffed turkey, and Maggie's visit wearing a silk negligee and red fur bedroom slippers.

"So you all had a pajama party?" he said with a chuckle.

"Hardly. But it was interesting in a way. Dorothy told me all about Reilly's hunting excursions. She said someone in his hunting parties usually gets hurt."

"Oh, yeah? What do you mean, 'hurt'?"

"Shot," Gretchen said bluntly. "Apparently Reilly shot someone on the last hunting trip."

Jarrod headed for the coffee pot. "Did they die?"

"Well, I don't really know. That's when Maggie arrived, and Dorothy left without finishing the story." In the middle of laying the dinner plates out on the dining table she suddenly stopped short. "Thank God you don't hunt, Jarrod."

"Me! I don't know any hunters. You say Dorothy's worried that Reilly's giving her a stuffed turkey for Christmas? Maybe Maggie wants one, too," he said with a laugh.

"It's not funny, Jarrod."

"Okay, it's not funny."

"And Jarrod . . . ?"

"Hmmm?"

"Just so you know, I do not want a stuffed turkey, or anything else stuffed in my living room. Ever."

He walked over and folded his arms around her. "Yeah, I know that."

"Thank you, honey."

He sniffed the air appreciatively. "By the way, what's for dinner?"

She could hardly get the words out. "Roast turkey. And stuffing."

Chapter Eight

# The Hairdresser

Gretchen turned into the mall and searched for a parking space close to Cut & Style, where she had a hair-cutting appointment that morning. Oh, good, a car was just pulling out of a space. She came to a stop and waited patiently, then out of the corner of her eye noticed something strange. Two men were crouching behind a white Mercedes, doing something to the license plate.

She pulled into the now-empty space and watched. Both men had long, unkempt hair, and one had tattoos all over his arm. With a start she realized they looked familiar, and an alarm bell went off in her brain. *Good Lord, that's Dale and Leonard Stanley. Those boys live right across the street from us!*

She reached into her purse for her cellphone, then realized she'd left it at home. Hurriedly she entered the hair salon and spoke to the first person she saw. "I'm Gretchen O'Malley. I have an eleven o'clock appointment, but first I need to use your telephone."

The woman smiled. "I'm Toni, Gretchen. Your appointment is with me."

"Oh, Toni, I just saw something I need to report to the police."

Toni's eyes widened. "Wow. What was it?" She led Gretchen to the cash register, where the telephone was.

"Something really strange is going on in the parking lot right outside," Gretchen said. "Two men with wrenches and a screwdriver are removing the license plate from a white Mercedes."

"Sounds like they're stealing it," Toni said. Anybody here own a white Mercedes?" she called out.

No response.

While Gretchen spoke to the 911 dispatcher, she glanced around the salon. The place was neat as a pin, with twelve hair-cutting stations, comfortable-looking black leather chairs, and large gold-framed mirrors. The walls were grey, which exactly matched the color of the ceramic sinks.

The dispatcher put her through to the police. "This is Mrs. Gretchen O'Malley," she said. "I'm at the mini-mall off of Robin Hood Boulevard, and I just saw two men take the license plate off a car. Yes, I recognized one of them. His name is Dale Stanley, and he lives on Sir Richard Road. But I wish to remain anonymous, since I live across the street from them."

When she hung up, Toni waved her over to a chair. Toni was older, maybe in her fifties, quite tall, with dyed blonde hair caught in a sort of bun on top of her head. "Now, let's get your hair washed before your cut."

Gretchen followed her to the line of sinks at the back of the salon, glad to sit down for a while. On the way she passed a man at one station, sitting with his back to her. My goodness, he was having his hair colored! He was also sipping a glass of wine, which she thought was an odd thing to be doing in a hair salon.

Suddenly she caught her breath. *That's my neighbor, Darrell Levine!* She scooted past him, but he looked up and saw her reflection in the mirror. Their eyes locked.

Instantly he turned away.

"Sit here, Gretchen," Toni instructed.

She slumped into the chair. "Oh my gosh," she whispered.

Toni stopped wetting her hair. "What's wrong?"

"I just saw my neighbor sitting in one of your chairs."

Toni shrugged. "Lots of people come to my salon, Gretchen. I'm glad you saw someone you know."

"But he's drinking a glass of wine!"

"Oh, that's Darrell. He's one of Sonja's regulars."

"But he's drinking alcohol!" Gretchen whispered. "He's a teetotaler, at least he says he is."

"Oh, Darrell always brings a bottle of wine with him when he comes in."

"But he's a Seventh Day Adventist. They don't drink alcohol."

Toni laughed. "I guess this one does."

"I wonder why a man his age would color his hair," Gretchen murmured.

"Maybe trying to recapture his youth," Toni said in a matter-of-fact tone. She caught Gretchen's gaze in the mirror and smiled. "Hairdressers keep all kinds of secrets," she whispered.

\*　　\*　　\*

When Gretchen returned home after a full day of errands, she got a real shock. There was that same white Mercedes, parked in front of the Stanley's house!

And there was Gladys in her driveway, with her binoculars trained on it.

Gretchen shook the matter out of her mind and started dinner. She was halfway through assembling a green salad when Jarrod burst into the kitchen. "Honey, you have to come into the living room!"

"Why? I'm just making my salad dressing."

"The police just drove up in front of the Stanley's house," he said. "Come and look."

Through the living room window she saw two shiny black patrol cars. "I wonder what's going on," Jarrod mused.

The neighbors started to gather across the street, watching, and then another squad car arrived. "Whoa," Jarrod exclaimed. "The whole neighborhood is out there! I'm going down and find out what's going on."

Gretchen dried her hands on a dishtowel and followed him. At the end of their driveway they met Reilly Hogan, from next door. "It's something about that Mercedes parked in front of the Stanley's," Reilly confided. "I heard one of the kids, Dale I think it was, yelling something about how they shouldn't have done it in Shellville. Can't help but wonder what he meant."

"Done what?" Jarrod asked. "What's 'it'?"

"Dunno." Reilly gestured. "The police and all the Stanleys are standing over there, in front of their garage."

Gretchen had just turned to look when angry male voices drifted from across the street.

"Damn it, Dale," his brother yelled. "Why didn't you put the damn car in the damn garage!"

"Me! Why should I? You were the one driving it."

"Calm down," one of the officers said. "Just keep it down, okay? Now then, tell me how you came into possession of this vehicle."

The neighbors began to edge closer.

"I didn't steal any damn car!" Dale shouted.

"Sir, this vehicle was reported stolen yesterday. Today it turns up here at your house. Can you explain this?"

Lucille Stanley started to cry. Larry stared at his sons, his face red and blotchy. "Tell him, Dale. Just tell him!"

"I didn't steal the car. I . . . bought it for my girlfriend."

"Then show us the registration and the bill of sale."

Larry smacked his son on one side of his head. "Do it, Dale. Show him!"

"No!" Dale shouted. "I don't have to show him. It's my car. I paid five thousand dollars for it, and it's mine. I don't have to prove it to anybody."

"I'm afraid you do, son," the officer said calmly. "We have a witness who says they saw you removing the license plate from this vehicle earlier today."

"Oh, yeah? Where?"

"In the parking lot at the mini-mall."

"I'll kill whoever called the police on me!" Dale yelled. "I swear I will."

Gretchen froze and stepped back behind Jarrod.

"Len, was it you that called them? Did ya do it just to make trouble for me?"

"Hell, no," Leonard shouted.

"Keep your voices down and stop using vulgar language," the officer said. "You're attracting a crowd."

"Hey," Leonard snapped. "Whose fault is that? We were just minding our own business when you barged in and started making accusations."

All at once Dale punched his brother in the stomach, doubling him over. "This is all your fault, Len."

"Dammit, Dale, wise up! It wasn't me who called the freakin' cops."

"That's it, fellas," the policeman said. "Cuff 'em," he called to his fellow officer.

Dale disappeared into one patrol car, Leonard into the second one. Larry and Lucille and the third son, Bruce, backed their beat-up Toyota out of the garage and sped down the street after the patrol cars while the neighbors stared.

"What did I tell you?" Reilly said. "Those kids are bad news. Bad, bad news."

Gretchen couldn't say a single word.

Just as all the commotion settled down and the neighbors began to drift off, Darrell Hogan and his wife walked up. Darrell's hair was a shiny rich shade of brown, Gretchen noted. And his once-grey eyebrows were the exact same color.

## Chapter Nine

## A Holly Jolly Christmas Party

The following week Gretchen and Jarrod headed to the DeCarrio's house for the appetizer phase of the Christmas progressive dinner. They walked briskly along in the chilly air until they came to the Stanley's house, but slowed when they heard loud voices coming from the open garage. Lucille's shrill voice rose into the night air.

"If you hadn't stolen that car, Dale, we would have been invited!"

"I didn't steal any car, Mom! The police let us go, didn't they?"

Jarrod took Gretchen's hand and they continued walking. "Guess the Stanleys won't be attending the progressive dinner," he remarked.

"Guess not," Gretchen agreed.

Jarrod rang the doorbell at the DeCarrio's, and they stood waiting in the entryway while deafening music poured from behind the door. After he rang the bell again, Gretchen said, "They can't hear it."

Jarrod nodded. "Sounds pretty rowdy in there. Maybe we should just walk in." He pushed the door open.

Gretchen gasped. Everyone was dressed in costume! Katalie waved at them. "Our new neighbors are here!" she shouted over the blaring music.

"Gosh," Gretchen whispered. "Their house layout is just like ours except for this brass stair railing and hardwood floor instead of carpeting." The living room, decorated in neutral tones of blue, beige, and eggshell white, overflowed with people, many of them neighbors she recognized.

"Did you know this was a costume party?" Jarrod murmured.

"No," she whispered. "Maybe that's what 'holiday dress' meant on the invitation."

Katalie swooped over and gave her a big hug. "Hi, you

guys! So glad you could come." She was dressed as a candy cane, complete with head-to-toe red and white stripes. "I made this outfit myself," she said proudly.

Gian Carlo was dressed as Santa Claus. He said nothing, just held up his wine glass with a big smile on his face.

A beautiful flocked Christmas tree decorated with shiny blue balls stood in the bay window. "Oh, how lovely!" Gretchen exclaimed.

"Yes, Katalie always has a beautiful tree," a voice said. A large green elf with a pointy hat and a black belt wrapped around her waist danced up, along with an oversized grey mouse whose face looked exactly like Marie Levine's. The elf looked like Dorothy Hogan.

Laughter drifted from the dining room. Gian Carlo handed Gretchen a glass of something with lots of ice cubes in it. "Try this. It's something special I came up with at our last party."

Gretchen took a tentative sip. "Wow, this is too strong for me."

"Let me get us some wine," Jarrod murmured. "I feel a bit

out of place." He caught Gretchen's eye and she smiled.

Katalie's cupboards, she noted, were stark white, as was her kitchen table. Bottles of liquor in all shapes and sizes filled every inch of the shiny surface. She sipped her wine and stared at the display. She saw no appetizers, just alcohol.

Marie approached, her long black mouse tail swishing around her feet. "Not in costume this evening?"

"No one told us about wearing costumes," Gretchen said.

"Oh. We always dress up at our Christmas parties. Guess you didn't get the message."

Tall, paunchy Tad Sabbin stood nearby, dressed as a toy soldier with black slacks, a smart red soldier's hat, and a crisp military jacket with a big white X on the front. "We got here an hour ago," he confided. His words were slurred. When Gretchen said nothing, he drifted over to Dorothy's husband, Reilly, and she couldn't help but overhear part of their conversation, something about shotguns. Apparently they were talking about hunting, and she tried to hear every word that was said, remembering Dorothy's tearful complaint about Reilly's fondness for stuffing the animals he killed. Reilly himself was dressed as a turkey, with flashing lights on his tail!

She pulled Jarrod away to the corner where Maggie and Chet stood, both dressed as Christmas packages. Maggie wore a huge sparkly bow on top of her head and sparkly white tights on her long legs. Her glittery red shoes had stiletto heels. Maggie did love her high heels! Chet had a matching sparkly bow on top of his head and silver glitter sprayed over his shoes.

Jazz poured out of a CD player, and two unidentified people disguised as Christmas trees were sassily dancing toward one another. "Those two are French exchange students who rent rooms at the DeCarrio's," Maggie whispered.

"Wait a minute," Jarrod said. "I thought zoning in this neighborhood prohibited renting out rooms."

"Yes, that's right," Maggie murmured. "I've gone down to the city and complained about it."

The two French-student Christmas trees were interrupted in their shimmying dance by toy-soldier Tad, who slipped an arm around one of them and leaned in close to whisper in her ear.

"Oh!" The girl jerked upright. "*Monsieur*, I will pretend I did not hear what you say. It is most improper!"

Tad stole a kiss and edged away, and the two Christmas trees resumed dancing, blowing kisses to Tad as he danced away.

"See what I mean?" Maggie intoned. "Not only that, those two are living here illegally. I think the tree with the angel on her head has something going on with Tad."

Maggie searched the room, murmuring, "Oh, poor Dana."

Gretchen found Jarrod in the living room. "What a party," she whispered.

"Wild," he muttered.

"It's almost seven o'clock," Katalie called out. "Time to go to Marie and Darrell's house for dinner, so drink up, everyone!"

Gretchen moved toward the door, but Jarrod was suddenly cornered by Reilly and a very intoxicated Tad. "It's just a quick day trip," Reilly said. "All the boys in the neighborhood go. It's a spot near the lake, about an hour's drive from here. You should come, Jarrod. We're going the week after Christmas."

To her horror, she heard her husband agree to go hunting

with Reilly. She headed back to the kitchen for another glass of wine, and when Jarrod joined her, she sent him a hard look. "It's just a day trip, honey," he protested. "What can happen on a day trip?"

Gretchen choked on her wine. *Plenty can happen, from what I've heard.*

Katalie shooed everyone out the front door, and a candy cane, a toy soldier, two Christmas packages, a mouse, an elf, and two Christmas trees staggered across the street. Gretchen took Jarrod's arm. "My word, this neighborhood does love to party!"

After a short walk, Marie Levine swung open her double front door to welcome the crowd. "Merry Christmas, everybody!" She was dressed as Raggedy Ann with an apron and thick red pigtails. Darrell, standing at the top of the stairs, made a burly Raggedy Andy with his hair and eyebrows colored jet black. His red wig sat sideways on his head.

The diners swarmed upstairs to the kitchen and grabbed dinner plates. Gladys appeared with two men wearing jogging suits, and suddenly there was Lucille Stanley, dressed as a

Christmas wreath! Gladys wore her usual winter sweatpants and furry hat with lights flashing around the edge. Her necklace also lights blinked on and off.

Suddenly Marie stiffened. "Oh, no. The Stanley boys are downstairs."

Gretchen blinked. "How do you know?"

She pointed to the security camera screen mounted on the counter near the stove. "It's wired for sound, so I can even hear what people are saying," she confided. She looked uneasy. "My son hooked it all up. Watch. If I turn it off, it looks just like a digital cookbook. Darrell has no idea it's there."

"Really," Gretchen said. Somehow having security cameras in one's house seemed, well, like an invasion of privacy. Especially if they were used to spy on one's husband.

"Now," Marie continued in a low voice, "I know all about everything Darrell does, about the hairdresser where he gets his hair colored. And Tad. I know all about him, too. Him and his little flirtations with younger women. Oh, God, Gretchen, it's so embarrassing."

"I thought Tad was married to Dana," Gretchen said.

"Oh, he is. But don't you remember? He lives on our street, and Dana lives in a separate house on Little John Way." She leaned closer. "Gretchen, the things I've seen from my front window would really upset Dana."

Gretchen then noticed a pair of binoculars sitting in plain view on the kitchen table. Wow! *Everyone in this neighborhood must have binoculars!* She pressed her lips together. This neighborhood was looking more and more strange. Weird, in fact.

Marie leaned toward her. "You know, Gretchen," she said confidentially. "Tad is the one who started Darrell going to the beauty shop. At first it was just to have his toenails clipped, but then the two of them started jogging, and they'd be gone all day. Then I found out that Darrell goes back to Tad's house and they . . . they drink! My husband is a Seventh Day Adventist and he's not supposed to use alcohol. But he drinks!"

"Um . . . to me, having a few glasses of wine here and there doesn't seem like the worst vice a man can have," Gretchen ventured.

"There's more." Marie rolled her eyes. "Tad's the one who is always talking about open marriage. He's a psychologist, and ... and he thinks it's okay to go to a beauty shop and encourage my husband to try to get his youth back."

Gretchen opened her mouth to reply, but Marie rushed on. "Tad tells him he looks awesome, twenty years younger. My God, he acts like a seventy-year-old fool who's trying to look twenty!"

Gretchen stared at her, unable to think of a single thing to say. Besides, she knew the security camera was taping everything, recording every move she made, every word she spoke. All at once she felt spied on. She couldn't wait to get out of Marie's house.

She eased over to Jarrod, who was talking to Chet by the fireplace near the large window that faced the street. "I'm ready for dessert," she breathed.

He drained the last of his drink. "Right."

On their way out, Gretchen noted that Marie had a bird's eye view of the entire neighborhood through her front window. In fact, *all* the front windows in every house she'd visited had clear views of everyone else's home.

Within the next ten minutes, the procession of Christmas elves and trees and Christmas packages lined the sidewalks, trooping back across the street where Reilly threw open his front door. "Welcome, everyone!"

Gretchen was at the back of the group of party-goers. All at once she looked across the street and saw someone sprint through the unlocked front door of the DeCarrio house.

"Jarrod," she whispered. "I just saw one of the Stanley boys, Dale, I think, sneak into Katalie and Gian Caro's house. Everybody is over here partying, so he's all alone in there." She made a beeline for Katalie, and Gian Carlo intercepted her. "You look worried about something, Gretchen. Don't you want any dessert?"

"Oh, yes, I do. It's just that . . ." She took a deep breath and explained about Dale.

Gian Carlo frowned, spun on his heel, and raced down the

stairs and out the front door.

*Well,* she thought, *I guess we'll find out soon enough what happened at the DeCarrio house.* She moved toward the dining room table, which was loaded with cakes and pies, and stopped short. There on the wall was the biggest stuffed elk head she'd ever seen. Its bulging brown eyes followed her as she backed away.

Jarrod was sipping some after-dinner brandy and eyeing the dessert table. "Jarrod, did you see that stuffed elk head mounted over the fireplace?"

"Sure did. What about all those stuffed mallards lined up on the mantel? And that huge black bear over there in the corner?"

Gretchen peered over her shoulder at the bear. "That's awful! Who would want all these dead animals in their home?"

"It's worse than awful. Look over there." He pointed to the center of the family room. "That's the biggest stuffed turkey I've ever seen. And in a glass display case."

"Dusting must be a nightmare for Dorothy," Gretchen murmured.

At that moment Reilly popped up beside them. "Admiring my turkey, huh?" He plunked down his dessert plate on top of the case and tapped the glass. "I got this baby with my first shot!"

Gretchen winced. "Where's Dorothy?" When Reilly shrugged, she went in search of her hostess and discovered that every single room had stuffed animals mounted on the walls or sitting in corners. There was even a stuffed skunk perched on top of a chest of drawers.

"And this isn't everything," Dorothy said from behind her.

Gretchen jumped. "Oh, you surprised me!"

"It's hideous, isn't it?" Dorothy said.

"Well, I-- I don't know what to say," Gretchen stammered.

"It started years ago and it's just gotten out of hand." Dorothy sounded as if she was about to cry.

"Don't you have a say about things in your own home?" Gretchen asked.

Dorothy snuffled. "Does it look like I do? Reilly has moved my sofa into the garage, and I don't think I can stand having that damn turkey in my family room. I think this is the last straw, Gretchen. The one that's going to break this camel's back."

"That big black bear looming in the corner would have done me in," Gretchen offered. The look on Dorothy's face warned her not to laugh. "Did you know that Reilly's talked Jarrod into going hunting with him next weekend?"

"Oh, no!" Dorothy clapped her hand over her mouth. "You have to stop him!"

"It's not like he's going to get shot or anything," Gretchen said weakly.

Dorothy's eyes widened. "Remind me to tell you what happened on another of Reilly's day trips last Aug— " She broke off when Gian Carlo suddenly appeared in the front doorway and began shouting.

"I just caught Dale Stanley trying to steal crystal glasses from our house! Everyone should go home right away and check your valuables!"

Dorothy looked at Gretchen. "What the heck happened at the DeCarrio's house?" She breezed past, leaving her standing in the hallway wondering what the heck happened on Reilly's hunting trip.

Chapter Ten

# The Bat

Gretchen watched her neighbors rush back to their homes to see if anything had been taken. "Sure is strange," she said while opening their front door, "how the party ended so abruptly."

"Yeah," Jarrod said.

"Oh, no!" She shot a look at him. "I left the front door unlocked."

"We'd better check to see if anything's missing," Jarrod said.

She walked to the china hutch, then checked the bookcase where Jarrod kept his coin collection. All there. She sighed in relief. "Just imagine, Jarrod, we live across the street from felons!"

"Check the bathroom medicine cabinet," he said.

She walked into the bedroom, then on into the bathroom.

"My medication is open and spread on the counter!"

"Did you leave it like that before we went to the party?"

"No! Do you think we should call the police?"

"Maybe we should get surveillance cameras," he said, looking at her.

"Oh, no. Those things creep me out."

"Huh? How come?"

She explained about Marie and Darrell's home surveillance system. "Marie can watch the whole neighborhood on her camera. It looks just like a cookbook on her kitchen counter, and Darrell doesn't even know."

"Calm down, honey." Jarrod wrapped his arms around her.

"The neighbors all have binoculars, too. They're all obviously watching out for something."

"Probably those Stanley boys," he said.

"Jarrod, let's ask the neighbors if anything is missing from their houses."

"Right." Gretchen followed him down the stairs and they walked to Reilly and Dorothy's house. The front door was standing open.

"Hello?" Jarrod called.

No answer.

They peeked inside. From the back of the house came the sound of a heated argument. "You just don't understand," Reilly was yelling. "We can't just move after the lawsuit. We can't afford it!"

Gretchen looked at her husband. "What lawsuit? Ring the doorbell, honey," she said quietly. Jarrod shook his head, and they started to go back down their stairs when Dorothy suddenly appeared in the hallway, wiping away tears.

"What are you guys doing here? Did you open my front door?"

"No," Gretchen said. "It was already open."

Dorothy's face was white as paste. "We were just arguing about the Stanley boys down the street. They're ruining our neighborhood."

"Is anything missing from your house?" Jarrod asked.

"Not that I've noticed yet," Dorothy replied. "What about

you?"

Gretchen nodded. "Some of my medication is missing."

Dorothy gasped. "Really?" Her eyebrows went up. "Oh, Dr. Ruggiero won't like that one bit. He has no tolerance for early prescription renewals."

"But someone took it!" Gretchen protested.

Dorothy tipped her head to one side. "Good luck with that one. You'd better call the police and report it and then take a copy of the police report to the doctor. It seems really odd that someone would take just some of the pills, not the whole bottle."

Gretchen stared at her. How odd that Dorothy would say that.

When they reached the sidewalk, a police squad car was parked in front of the DeCarrio's house and their front door stood wide open. They could hear Gian Carlo shouting at the police inside.

"Excuse us," Jarrod said loudly. "Our house has been broken into."

The two police officers, one tall and thin and the other

heavier, waved for them to come in. "Looks like more than a few homes have been robbed. We're almost finished here," the tall officer said. "We'll take your statement and check out your home."

"My grandmother's crystal vases are missing," Gian Carlo said in his thick Italian accent. "And they got into our medicine cabinet."

After an hour, Jarrod and Gretchen showed the officers the pills spread out on their bathroom counter.

"Do you have camera surveillance?" he asked.

"No."

"Too bad. All your neighbors have surveillance. Makes it easier to identify the culprits."

"How many houses have been broken into?" Jarrod asked.

"Four, so far," the officer replied. "Valuable tools are missing, along with fine crystal glass and prescription medications."

"Let me check my garage," Jarrod said. "I have lots of valuable old tools."

One of the officers followed him downstairs, and when they returned Jarrod sent Gretchen a pained look. "Dad's old wooden plane is gone. And his toolbox."

"What are the chances of getting those things back?" she asked the officer.

"Not good. Unless we can find the items in the thief's possession. We have two boys and their father in for questioning at the station right now."

*　　*　　*

Gretchen rolled over and shook her husband awake. "Jarrod! Did you hear that car door slam? It sounded like it was in front of our house."

Jarrod crawled out of bed. "I'll take a look."

She glanced at the clock. It was two in the morning.

Jarrod peered out the front window. "Honey, a police car is parked in front of Dorothy and Reilly's house."

Gretchen tied her bathrobe and peered over his shoulder. "What's going on?"

Jarrod grabbed his coat and slippers and raced downstairs.

Peeking between the living room blinds, Gretchen watched another squad car pull up and neighbors begin spilling out of their houses.

"Do you know what happened?" Gian Carlo yelled to Jarrod."

Gretchen decided to join them, bathrobe or not. "What's going on?"

"Something about a bat," Jarrod answered.

"A bat? You mean a baseball bat?"

"Yeah."

"Is someone hurt?" she asked.

Suddenly Reilly stumbled out of his house, visibly upset. A police officer was patting his shoulder. "It's just a bird," he said. "You can always shoot another one."

The officer pulled out his ledger. "What happened?"

Reilly groaned. "My wife and I went to bed, and the next thing I knew I heard glass breaking and some pounding. Dorothy was in the family room, screaming something about being god-awful ugly and the last straw. When I rushed in there she was, beating the hell out of my stuffed turkey. My beautiful stuffed turkey. Glass was flying all over the place. I tried to stop her, but . . ." He swallowed hard.

Gretchen turned away and began to laugh, covering her mouth so no one could hear. Jarrod gave her a sharp look. "What's so funny?" he intoned.

She couldn't answer. *So Dorothy got rid of the stuffed turkey . . . her way.*

"Mr. Hogan," the police officer said, "Do you want to press charges?"

"No!" Reilly yelled. "I didn't call you! I don't know why you came. This is between my wife and me."

"Who called the police?" Gretchen whispered. Gian Carlo and Jarrod looked at each other. Gretchen peered into the back yard, and there was Gladys, standing on her deck with her fuzzy hat, her coat on over her pajamas, and binoculars held up to her eyes. Her other hand gripped her clipboard.

Across the street, Lucille and Larry Stanley, still dressed in their party clothes, started toward them. "It's awful to have the police just appear at your house," Lucille said, her voice strident.

Gretchen and Jarrod looked at each other. Then Dorothy appeared in her driveway, wearing a bathrobe and carrying a baseball bat. She looked calm and collected.

Gretchen leaned toward Jarrod. "She looks happy about what she did."

"I think we should leave them alone to work it out," Jarrod said quietly.

As they moved away, Gretchen overheard one police officer say to Dorothy, "I think we should take the bat, Mrs. Hogan."

Dorothy just smiled and handed it over. Gretchen had to grit her teeth to keep from laughing. She imagined Dorothy beating the stuffed bird and Reilly looking on in horror. *Good for her! She got rid of the turkey.*

"Why are you laughing?" Jarrod asked when they got home.

"Oh, honey, Dorothy hated that stuffed turkey. Hated it!"

He chuckled. "You mean that turkey was what sent Dorothy over the edge?"

"Exactly."

Jarrod yawned. "This has been some night! First the party, then the break-ins and robberies, and now Dorothy and the turkey. I won't be able to sleep."

"Gladys was watching it all in her back yard with her binoculars and her clipboard, but I wonder who called the police?"

"Don't know. Don't care."

"Honey?"

"Yes?" he said with a yawn.

"When we were looking at the house, didn't this look like a nice, quiet neighborhood?"

"Yeah, sure did." He crawled into bed. "But now we know. And tomorrow, we're getting a surveillance camera."

Chapter Eleven

## Only Her Hairdresser Knows for Sure

On Thursday Gretchen drove to Cut & Style Hair Salon to have her hair colored. She parked her car and walked past the bookstore to the shop, where Toni greeted her. "Hi, Gretchen. You're right on time. How are you?"

Gretchen plopped down in the chair with a sigh. "It's been kind of a crazy time."

Toni caught her eye in the mirror. "Oh? I'll mix up your color and you can tell me about it."

Five minutes later Gretchen folded her hands under the hairdresser's drape and met Toni's gaze. "Well, remember those fellows I saw removing the license plate from that car on my last visit? I think I told you those boys were my neighbors."

"Yes, you did." She sectioned off part of Gretchen's hair. "Is there more?"

"There sure is. The police came, and all the neighbors gathered in the street, and then a fight broke out between the brothers. The police took them both off to the police station."

Toni shook her head. "Wow."

"But that was nothing compared to what happened at our Christmas block party."

"You mean the burglary?"

Gretchen stared at her. "You know about that? How did you know about what happened during the block party?"

"Another one of my clients lives next door to you."

"Who? Maggie Gaines or Dorothy Hogan?"

Toni hesitated. "Well, I just did Dorothy's hair."

Gretchen snapped her mouth closed. "And she told you all about our robberies?" *This is a really small, gossipy town.*

"Dorothy told me how terrible it was that everyone in the neighborhood had something stolen, including her."

"What was stolen from Dorothy?" she inquired.

"Medication prescribed from her doctor. Her entire prescription. You know Dorothy has bad knees?"

"No," Gretchen murmured, "I didn't know."

"Yes. Dorothy works as a receptionist for the doctor. He gave her a really hard time because this same thing has happened to her before."

Gretchen sighed. "There doesn't seem to be much that's private in this town."

Toni paused to catch Gretchen's eye in the mirror. "Do you like your neighbors?"

"Yes," Gretchen lied. *Well, maybe not all of them. Some of them are really strange.*

Toni changed the subject. "So, what are your plans for the New Year?"

"Just getting settled in our new home. And seeing my parents."

"That's nice. Your color needs to process, so I'll be back in twenty minutes."

Gretchen settled down to wait and glanced at the woman in the next chair. It was Sandra Livingston, from the bookstore. "Oh, hello, Sandra."

"Hi. I remember you. You bought "The Help" at the bookstore, right?"

"Right."

"I couldn't help overhearing about your neighborhood robbery. Did you have anything stolen?"

"Yes, I had some prescription medication taken."

Sandra shook her head sympathetically. "Do they know who did it?"

"I think so."

"That's good. My husband said a whole neighborhood got robbed when they got together for a block party, and now he's having to refill a lot of prescriptions. He's not too happy about that."

"Your husband? Is he a physician?"

"Dr. Ruggiero is my husband. I know, my name is Livingston; that's because I kept my maiden name."

Toni returned just as Sandra left the shop. "I see you met the bookstore owner. You know she's writing a book about our little town."

Gretchen jerked. "No, I didn't know. I hope I won't be in it. I really value my privacy."

She scanned the shop. Before she said another word she wanted to be sure there was no one she knew who might overhear.

## Chapter Twelve

## **Surveillance**

After leaving the hair salon, Gretchen started to get in her Lexus when she spied Sandra and Annie Blumme standing in the doorway of Blumme's florist. "Hi, you two!" Gretchen called with a smile. They stopped talking abruptly. Annie folded her arms across her middle and smiled, but Sandra studied her carefully.

"Hello," they said in unison.

"Fancy running into you twice today," Gretchen said to Sandra.

Annie flicked Sandra a glance. "I saw Gretchen today at the beauty shop," Sandra explained.

"Oh," Annie said. "I should make an appointment to get mine done."

Sandra nodded. "Gretchen, have you spoken to my husband

about your prescription yet?"

"Well, no, not yet."

Sandra glanced at Annie. "Gretchen lives in the neighborhood that had the burglaries," she said.

Annie unfolded her arms. "Gretchen sees your husband, here in town?"

"Yes, she does," Sandra replied.

Gretchen tensed. *Who my doctor is, is no one's business but mine. I'm not going to discuss my medical issues with people I hardly know.*

She excused herself and walked into Val's Grocery Store, and by the time she reached the produce department and picked up fresh green beans and salad makings for dinner, she'd started to cool off. At the meat counter, the butcher smiled at her.

"How are you today, Mrs. O'Malley?"

"Fine. I'd like some fresh salmon, please."

"Sure thing. I heard about your Thanksgiving dinner. Good thing there was no real damage."

Gretchen didn't really want her Thanksgiving disaster talked about, but she guessed the butcher was just being friendly. Then out of the corner of her eye she noticed a woman peering into her grocery cart.

"Oh, Maggie! Hello." *Goodness, I'm running into everyone today.* She moved the cart away from Maggie.

Maggie grinned at her. "What's for dinner tonight?"

"Salmon."

"Yum. That sounds good. Ralph, I'll have a pound of salmon, too."

The butcher nodded.

Maggie touched her arm. "Guess what, Gretchen? I just ran into Sandra Livingston and Annie Blumme. You do know they're related to each other, don't you?" She pulled a tube of lipstick from her purse.

"No, I didn't know that.

"Oh, yes. Annie and her husband, Max, live on Maid Marian Street. Her husband is a doctor over in Breyerville. An internal medicine doctor, like Sandra's husband."

Gretchen nodded.

"Annie and Max were supposed to come to our block Christmas party, but they had other plans. Now they're happy they didn't come because all our houses were broken into." She moved closer to Gretchen. "I saw a surveillance systems truck in front of your house just now."

"You did? Jarrod must be looking into getting a surveillance camera for our house."

"Oh, we all have surveillance cameras, you know," Maggie said with a smile.

The butcher handed Gretchen the wrapped salmon, and Gretchen put it in her grocery cart and moved away. "I need to run, Maggie. Have to start dinner."

When she turned onto Sir Richard Road, she saw a large white van parked in front of her house. Safety First Surveillance Systems. Oh, Lord, Jarrod was really serious about getting a surveillance camera! She grabbed the grocery bag and went inside.

She hated surveillance cameras. They were intrusive. She liked nice, quiet neighborhoods, and privacy.

As she was setting the kitchen table for dinner, she glanced out the window to see Gladys training her binoculars on the house.

"She doesn't miss anything that goes on," Jarrod said from behind her. "She's probably writing down the license number of the van and a description of the guy that sold us the system."

Gretchen sighed. "Oh, Jarrod, I really dislike surveillance systems."

"Seriously, Gretch, this whole neighborhood is wired. The guy who installed our system put in the same system for Maggie and Chet and Marie and Darrell and even the Stanleys. All of them can see more than just what happens around their own houses."

She shot him an accusing look. "What does that mean?"

"They're all wired for sound and distance, and they can see the whole neighborhood on their television sets."

"What? From their TV's?"

"That's what the installer guy said. And if the system is set up correctly, we can all listen to each other's conversations."

"No!" Gretchen shouted. "Jarrod, this is terrible! Why would we want to do that?"

He studied the platter of salmon steaks she set on the table. "I'm guessing because of the boys across the street."

Gretchen pushed her plate away. "I am not happy about this, Jarrod."

"I know."

"I wish we had known about those Stanley boys before we moved in."

Jarrod didn't respond, and they ate in silence. Finally he laid down his fork. "Come on, Gretchen, why are you so upset?"

She drew in a long breath. "Well, to begin with we have neighbors who seem to want to know everything about each other. Then there are the Stanley boys. And I am finding out how small this town really is. Everybody knows everybody else or they're related or . . ."

"Well, it's a small town, honey. It's what we wanted."

She blew her nose. "You know that new doctor I have?"

"Yeah, what about him?"

"His wife is Sandra Livingston, who owns the bookstore. She's related to Annie Blumme, who owns the florist shop."

"So? Why is that important?"

"Sandra overheard me talking to my hairdresser today, about my medication being stolen during the block party. She asked me all sorts of personal questions. And Dr. Ruggiero is Sandra's husband!"

"Whew," Jarrod muttered. "Word seems to spread around fast in this town."

"It's more than that, Jarrod. This is a *medical* issue. Medical issues are private matters. It's bad enough that Dorothy Hogan works for Dr. Ruggiero; now his wife knows all about me, too."

"You could change doctors, couldn't you?"

She pressed her lips together. "I could if I wanted to drive out of town. But that's a lot of driving."

"Looks like things are different here in Shellville."

Gretchen stood up and put her plate in the sink. "They sure are different here. And I'm not so sure I like it."

Chapter Thirteen

# Doctor's Appointment

On the morning of her appointment with Dr. Ruggiero, Gretchen dressed tastefully in black wool slacks and a long-sleeved turquoise sweater, then added gold earrings and a gold bracelet Jarrod had given her on her birthday. Mr. Parker, their Yorkshire terrier, knew she was going out and paced back and forth at the front door.

"Mr. Parker, kennel," she ordered. "I'll take you for a walk when I get home."

When she backed out of the driveway she caught sight of a work crew at Maggie and Chet's house. Were they replacing their front door? Or remodeling? The garage door was open at Dorothy's house; however, there were no cars.

But there was Gladys, sitting outside in her chair in front of her garage with a heat lamp next to her feet, her ever-present clipboard in her lap. Gretchen waved, but Gladys was peering through her binoculars when she drove by. *Good old predictable Gladys. I'd dearly love to read what she writes down on that clipboard of hers.*

Twenty minutes later, she walked into Dr. Ruggiero's office to find a waiting room full of people. At the receptionist's desk she stood behind an older woman on crutches while Dorothy arranged files and talked on the phone.

"Hi, Gretchen," she called. "That's my new neighbor," she announced. "She has a problem with her blood pressure." Then she lowered her voice. "Doctor is running a bit behind, so take a seat." She turned to answer another phone call and waved Gretchen and the older woman away.

Gretchen took a seat between a grey-haired man and a woman with short frizzy white hair who looked to be his wife. "I've been waiting over an hour," she whispered.

An hour! She flipped through magazines until she heard Dorothy's voice. "Gretchen O'Malley. The doctor will see you now about that prescription you lost."

*What? I didn't lose it; it was stolen!*

Dorothy pointed to a room at the end of the hallway. "The nurse is out sick, so no need to check your weight or your blood pressure. And I already noted that you lost your medication."

"I didn't lose it, Dorothy. It was stolen, remember?"

The door clicked shut and Dorothy was gone. Ten minutes passed and finally tall, gray-haired Dr. Ruggiero appeared. "I just saw you two weeks ago, didn't I?" he said, looking up from her chart.

"Yes, you did."

"And you need more blood pressure medication, is that it?"

"Yes. We had a robbery, and my medicine cabinet was rifled. They took almost all my pills."

Dr. Ruggiero frowned. "Anything else?"

"Well, yes. Old tools that belonged to my husband's father."

"Hmmm." He leaned back and stroked his chin. "Well, I guess your story adds up."

"What does that mean? What story? That's what happened. Other people had things stolen that same night." She dug in her purse until she found the police report, unfolded it and handed it to him.

"Whoa," he exclaimed. "Half these people are patients of mine. Marie and Darrell Levine were in yesterday for more of their medication. They both have rheumatoid arthritis. And Maggie Gaines . . . well, Maggie has mysterious things happen to her. Last year she injured her back and was in a wheelchair for a month. We thought it was MS, but it turned out to be a nerve problem." He cleared his throat. "But back to the robberies. I heard about them from one of my neighbors, Edgar Langley. He's a police officer. He was in for shoulder surgery last year."

Gretchen could scarcely believe her ears. Was he really telling her about his other patients? She stared at him as he took out his pen and prescription pad.

"Dorothy lost her entire prescription," he muttered. "She has two very bad knees that need replacing, but she can't afford it right now. She's trying to settle a messy lawsuit with one of her neighbors."

"What? Isn't that a private matter?"

He didn't answer. Instead, he handed her the prescription and replaced the pen in his pocket. "You need to lock up your medications, not just store them in your bathroom medicine cabinet. I told all your neighbors the same thing. By the way, I'd like to make a copy of this police report. You're the only one of my patients who got one."

Gretchen blinked. "How could you possibly know that?"

"My receptionist. Dorothy keeps up on everything." He moved to the door. "Come back in six months, Mrs. O'Malley."

Her visit to Dr. Ruggiero's office was unsettling, to say the least. She slid into the Lexus and had just started the engine when she looked in the rear view mirror to see Dorothy waving at her. She rolled down the window.

"Your new appointment card," Dorothy panted. "Be sure to tear up your old one."

Gretchen bit her lip. What an odd thing to say. She wasn't a child or feeble-minded, so why remind her to tear up the old card? She put the remark out of her mind, drove to the pharmacy to fill the prescription, and then went home to walk Mr. Parker.

With the terrier on his leash, Gretchen had just started past Maggie and Chet's house when she heard someone call her name. "Gretchen!" Maggie shouted from her front porch. "Could you take Charlie along with you?"

"Um, well actually I don't feel comfortable walking someone else's dog, Maggie."

"Oh. Then I guess I'll just have to walk him myself tonight." She disappeared through her front door and Gretchen and Mr. Parker walked on. When she turned the corner she noticed Dorothy's garage door was still open.

Then she caught sight of Gladys, still sitting in front of her garage. She tugged on Mr. Parker's leash and started toward her, but suddenly Gladys leaped up and sprinted down the street.

*What on earth? Where is she going in such a hurry?*

After a long walk in the park, she and Mr. Parker returned home to find Jarrod glued to the living room window.

"Did you see the police over at the Stanley house?" he asked.

"No. I've been walking the dog in the park."

"Three squad cars are out front. Come and look." He made room for her at the window.

Gladys was standing between their house and Maggie and Chet's, her binoculars trained on the Stanley residence.

"I'll go down and ask Gladys," Jarrod said. "She knows everything going on in the neighborhood."

He was gone a long time, long enough for Gretchen to have dinner on the table when he returned. His face looked odd, as if he'd had a shock. "Jarrod? What's going on?"

He sat down heavily at the dining table. "Larry Stanley is dead."

Gretchen dropped her fork. "What? How could that be? He wasn't sick, was he?"

"I don't know anything except what Gladys told me. Lucille is home, but Gladys doesn't know where the boys are. The police are there, too."

"Why?"

"Gladys said one of them took a rifle out of the house."

"Oh, my God. You don't think— ?"

Jarrod shrugged. "Wish I knew, honey. Did you see anything strange when you were out walking the dog?"

"Well, I ran into Maggie on my way to the park. And Gladys," she added. "But Gladys raced off somewhere before I could speak to her."

"The police are questioning all the neighbors," her husband said. "They'll probably come over to talk to us, too."

"Jarrod?" she asked quietly. "It's possible there's been a murder. Is our surveillance camera working?"

Chapter Fourteen

## What She Saw

At ten o'clock that night the doorbell rang. Jarrod switched off the TV, and he and Gretchen found a police officer standing on the porch. After establishing how long they had lived in the neighborhood, and how well they knew the Stanleys, the officer turned to Gretchen.

"Where were you today, Mrs. O'Malley?"

"I was at my doctor's this morning. Then I came home and walked my dog in the park."

"Did you see anything out of the ordinary?"

"Only that our neighbors in the corner house had their garage door open all day, but the cars were gone."

"Did you see Maggie or Chet Gaines?" he asked.

"I saw Maggie when I took the dog for a walk," Gretchen said. "She was standing in front of the stairs going up to her house."

"Was she coming or going?"

She shot the officer a quick look. "Oh, I don't know. She wanted me to take her dog for a walk, but I said I couldn't, so she walked into her house and shut the door."

"Did you see anyone else from the neighborhood on your walk?"

"Yes. An older woman who lives on the street behind us. Her name is Gladys. She was sitting in front of her garage." Gretchen purposely didn't mention the binoculars or the clipboard.

"Did you speak to her?"

"No. She raced off before I could say anything. She disappeared between two houses and I lost track of her."

The policeman frowned and jotted something down. "What time did you return home?"

"I don't know, exactly. Around dinnertime. Jarrod told me there was a police car in front of the Stanley's house."

"Had either of you called them?"

"No!" Jarrod and Gretchen said in unison.

The officer looked up from his notes. "Mrs. O'Malley, someone reported that you called in a disturbance in the neighborhood around five o'clock."

"But I didn't!"

"And Mr. O'Malley, you were alone here in the house until your wife got home?"

"Yes."

"Do you have a surveillance camera?"

"Yes," Jarrod said. "I just had it installed yesterday."

"We may need to view your tape from today, so don't do anything with it."

"Officer, what exactly has happened?"

He shook his head. "I'm not at liberty to say, but you know that Larry Stanley is dead."

Gretchen shut her eyes. "This is awful," she said. "How did he die?"

"I'm sorry, ma'am, I can't tell you that."

"Are we safe here in our neighborhood?" Jarrod asked.

"Probably," the policeman said. "But keep your doors locked and keep an eye out. Call us if anything looks out of the ordinary."

Gretchen choked back a laugh. "To tell the truth, officer, there hasn't been anything ordinary about this neighborhood since the day we moved in."

\*    \*    \*

At six the following morning the phone rang. Gretchen rolled over in bed. "Doesn't anyone in this neighborhood ever sleep?"

Jarrod picked up the phone, then passed it to her. "It's Dorothy."

Gretchen cleared her throat. "Dorothy, we're not up yet. Can I call you back?"

Dorothy's voice sounded brittle. "I'm standing right outside your front door. I need to talk."

Gretchen sat up. "I'll be right down."

Dorothy looked as if she hadn't slept. Her hair was uncombed, and her clothes were wrinkled. "Did you hear?" she asked.

"Hear what?"

"The police found one of Reilly's rifles at the Stanley's house." She began to cry.

"S-someone broke into our house yesterday and s-stole it."

Gretchen touched her shoulder. "Have the police told you how Larry died?"

"Oh, God, isn't that obvious?" Dorothy snuffled.

Gretchen bit her lip. "No, not to me. Do you know?"

Dorothy hesitated.

"Dorothy, come on in. I'll make some coffee." While she opened the blinds and started the coffeemaker, Dorothy sank heavily into a chair at the kitchen table and dropped her head into her hands. "Last night the police were at our house for hours, counting all Reilly's guns and rifles and checking his permits."

"That must have been very unsettling," Gretchen said. She wiped up some milk she'd spilled on the counter and put the milk carton back in the refrigerator.

Suddenly Dorothy let out a squeal. "There's Gladys!" She

pointed out the window. "She spies on everybody all day long. Maybe she saw who was in our garage yesterday."

"Don't you have a surveillance camera?"

"Yes, but someone had disconnected it."

"Did the police check it? They should be able to see who disconnected it."

Dorothy shook her head. "I don't know. They took our video down to the police station, but we haven't heard anything."

When Jarrod came downstairs, Dorothy finished the last of her coffee and left. When Gretchen offered to make breakfast, he shook his head. "I have an early appointment, honey. Lock the doors if you leave the house." He opened the refrigerator and gave her an odd look.

"Is this your new place to store dishtowels?" He pulled out a towel and laid it on the counter.

"Oh." She sent him an apologetic smile. "I spilled some milk and . . . Jarrod, I'm not thinking too clearly. I'm really nervous about what's going on in our neighborhood."

"Yeah." He patted her shoulder. "Remember to keep the

door locked."

Chapter Fifteen

## What Really Happened?

That morning after Jarrod left for work, Gretchen locked the front door, attached Mr. Parker's leash, and started walking around the cul-de-sac. The entire neighborhood seemed oddly quiet, and she looked carefully at the houses as she passed. Marie Levine was peering out her living room window, but when Gretchen waved, Marie disappeared. *That's strange. Why didn't she wave back at me?*

She walked on to discover Lucille Stanley sitting on her door step, in tears. The tall woman stood up and walked listlessly toward her. Gretchen noted that her face looked ravaged, her skin pale and her eyes red and swollen. She stepped forward and touched her arm.

"Lucille, I am so sorry to hear about Larry."

Lucille drew in a long, shaky breath. "You know, my boys

went to private schools, didn't you? Larry and I did the best we could in raising them. They're really good kids."

"I'm sure you and Larry did a good job, Lucille. Raising kids isn't easy."

"Sure, they made some bad choices," the woman went on. "What kids don't make mistakes?"

Gretchen didn't know what to say, so she just nodded.

"Larry died of a heart attack," Lucille announced. "Did you know that?"

"No, I did not know that."

"I heard the neighborhood rumors, that Larry was murdered." Lucille scanned the houses bordering the cul-de-sac. "These people never made an effort to get to know us."

Gretchen stared at her. She hadn't been living here long enough to know whether that was true or not.

"Just because the police found someone's rifle in our garage doesn't mean my boys put it there, does it?" Lucille asked in a low voice.

"No, of course not," Gretchen murmured.

"I called the police when we found it."

Gretchen stepped closer. "Lucille, please let me know if there is anything I can do, okay?"

"Okay. Thanks, Gretchen. I really appreciate that."

She watched Lucille move back to her front steps, then continued walking Mr. Parker. She hadn't gone half a block when Maggie and her big black Labrador came around the corner.

"I saw you talking to Lucille," Maggie said. "I stayed out of sight."

"Why would you do that?"

Maggie tossed her head. "I want nothing to do with the Stanleys. They're all bad eggs."

"Maggie, wait a minute. Lucille has just lost her husband. She deserves our sympathy."

"Oh, for God's sake, Gretchen, one of her kids killed Larry! Who's going to be next?"

Gretchen frowned at that. "Before you spread that around, I think you should check it out with Lucille."

"What? What did she tell you?"

"Maggie, I am not saying anything to anyone until the police investigation is concluded. Lucille and her boys deserve the benefit of the doubt."

Maggie yanked her dog's leash. "You better be careful whose side you choose, Gretchen."

"What?" Gretchen studied her angry expression. "Maggie, what is that supposed to mean?"

"It means just what I said," Maggie snapped. She jerked the leash again and stomped on down the sidewalk with her Labrador. Gretchen watched her for a moment, then headed in the opposite direction toward Little John Way, and turned the corner.

Oh, good heavens, there was Gladys! This time she wasn't looking through her binoculars; she was talking to Dana Sabbin and Marie Levine. Dana looked as if she was crying. Gladys was scribbling on her clipboard.

Gretchen moved toward them and smiled. "Good morning. How are you both today?"

Dana swiped tears off her cheeks. "The police just took Tad down to the police station for questioning. And they wouldn't let me come with him!"

"Did they say why?"

"It has something to do with one of the girls who live at the DeCarrio's. And one of Reilly Hogan's rifles that was found in the Stanley's garage."

"Why, that's terrible," Gretchen said. "I am so sorry."

"Tad goes hunting with Reilly once in a while," Dana continued. "And on the last trip, one of those girls went along. Chet Gaines got shot in the butt, and the next thing we knew there was a lawsuit, and then the rifle that shot Chet went missing."

Gretchen opened her mouth to speak, but Dana wasn't finished. "Larry Stanley found that rifle in his garage. All I know is that Dorothy Hogan shouldn't let her husband take anyone hunting with him because mysterious accidents always happen. One of these days someone is going to get killed."

Gretchen said nothing. Larry Stanley was dead. Maybe it

was a heart attack, as his wife said. Or maybe he was shot. Either way, she wasn't going to comment until all the facts were known. *And if Maggie doesn't like it, that's tough!*

*     *     *

Gretchen set two dinner plates on the dining table and shot a glance at Jarrod, in front of the TV. "You know, Jarrod, I felt really sorry for Lucille today."

He switched off the sound. "Yeah, I can imagine."

"The neighbors don't really know what happened to Larry, and I'm not about to tell any of them what Lucille told me."

"Good idea, honey. Stay out of it. But just between us, what do you think really happened?"

"Just between us, Jarrod, Dana had some interesting information. She hinted that one of those girls living at the DeCarrio's house had gone hunting with Reilly Hogan. Dana thinks maybe this girl had something to do with the rifle the police found in the Stanley's garage."

Her husband looked up. "How does she know that?"

"Well, she doesn't, really. I think she's just guessing. Or

maybe there were some fingerprints. It's also possible that Dana is making illogical connections."

"Right. The police wouldn't say anything about rifles or fingerprints or anything about their investigation while it's ongoing."

Gretchen opened the refrigerator and took out her green salad. "Exactly. And neither should anyone else."

Jarrod turned the TV off and sat staring at the blank screen. "The whole thing is strange, Gretch. Kinda makes you wonder which of our neighbors is trying to hide what, doesn't it?"

She gave him a startled look. "Let's eat dinner and try not to think about it."

Jarrod smacked a kiss on her cheek. "You're one smart lady, you know that?"

Gretchen sighed. Yes, she knew that. She'd always been aware of what went on around her. Her mother used to say she missed nothing.

But lately she found herself wishing that she wasn't quite so observant.

Chapter Sixteen

# Watching Real TV

By Saturday morning Gretchen had to get away from the house, away from the neighborhood and the vague feeling of unease that settled over her the minute she opened her eyes each morning. When Jarrod announced he was going to the hardware store for a box of nails and some cabinet drawer pulls, she decided to go along. A cup of coffee and a quiet half hour at Strudel Bakery might help restore her sense of balance.

Jarrod dropped her off and she splurged on a pumpkin-spice latte and a scone and chose a corner seat near the back. She had no sooner taken a sip of her coffee when she heard Dorothy Hogan's voice arguing with someone.

"They already got a load of our money," she said angrily. "Oh, I wish I'd never moved to that damn neighborhood in the first place!"

Gretchen turned around to see Dorothy sitting across from a heavyset man with a fringe of grey hair and round black glasses. Dorothy was frowning at him, and her mouth was pressed in a thin line.

In the next moment the door banged open and in walked Maggie. Gretchen waved her over.

"I can't stop," Maggie said. "I came in to meet with Dorothy."

Gretchen pointed to the back table. "She's over there."

"Oh. My goodness, she's sitting with my attorney!"

"Your attorney?"

"Yes. *My* attorney, not Dorothy's. It's a complicated mess, but it's almost resolved. Or it will be very soon."

At that moment Dorothy made a beeline for Maggie, pointing her finger at her. "What are you going to do with all that money you're getting from us, huh? Huh, Maggie? Chet didn't even get a hole in his pants where the bullet supposedly grazed him, and now you . . . you're s-suing us for pain and suffering?"

Maggie took a step backward, but apparently Dorothy

wasn't finished. Her face twisted in a scowl. "I know you've sued someone else in the neighborhood. No wonder you and Chet don't need to work!"

The attorney lurched to his feet and stepped in between the two women. Maggie elbowed past him. "You know, Dorothy, when you're being sued, you can't talk about the case. That's what a 'nondisclosure clause' means."

"I'll talk if I want to!"

Gretchen watched in disbelief. Multiple lawsuits? Why in heaven's name would Maggie and Chet sue their neighbors? *What was wrong with them?* She concentrated on finishing her latte and her scone and tried to shut out the voices. After a few minutes she tossed the rest of her coffee and the half-eaten scone into the trash can, left the bakery, and hurried over to the hardware store.

Jarrod caught sight of her through the window and walked outside. "Honey, why are you pacing back and forth out here?" He touched her shoulder.

"Oh my gosh, Jarrod, I just found out something really

surprising. Maggie and Chet are suing Dorothy and Reilly, and apparently it's not the first time they have sued some of our neighbors."

"What?"

"It's true. I just overheard Dorothy confront Maggie in the bakery. Dorothy was shouting, all about that's how Maggie can afford to live in our neighborhood, by suing people!"

"I think we'd better steer clear of them," Gretchen said.

"Hard to do, since they're our next-door neighbors."

That didn't make her feel any better. They drove home in silence, and when they reached Robin Hood Boulevard, Gretchen spied Gladys standing in her driveway with her binoculars trained on Maggie's house. The grey-haired woman motioned for them to be quiet.

Gretchen rolled down her window. "What's going on, Gladys?"

"Shh! I'm trying to hear what's happening."

"Where? At Maggie's house?"

"Yes."

"I don't see Maggie anywhere," Gretchen pointed out.

"Exactly!" Gladys turned and disappeared behind Maggie and Chet's house.

Jarrod slammed the car door. "I think our neighbors are nuts!"

"Which ones?" she said dryly.

"All of them." He unlocked the front door and headed for his workshop. Gretchen went downstairs to the family room, but before she reached it she heard a tap on the window. Out of the corner of her eye she saw a small boy peering in.

"What are you doing here?" Gretchen yelled.

The boy pointed down the street, and Gretchen rushed to the front door to see what was going on. A tall, thin young woman walked up on the porch and smiled at her. She had dark brown hair and brown eyes and was wearing jeans and a red Nike tee shirt. I'm Holly," she explained. "I met you at the Christmas block party."

Gretchen frowned. "Are you sure?"

"Oh, yes. I was one of the Christmas trees!"

Gretchen smiled. "Ah. I remember now. You were dancing with another tree."

Holly laughed. "I have a favor to ask. Could you watch my son, James, for a short time? I have to go down to the police station."

"When?" Gretchen blurted. "You mean now?"

"Yes, now." Holly gave her a tentative smile. "I'll only be gone for an hour or so. I know it's an odd request, but James is easily entertained. You could watch him at my house where he has his toys and his videos."

"Well . . ."

"Please?" she pleaded. "I already tried everyone else in the neighborhood, but nobody is home this morning."

Gretchen sighed, locked her door, and followed Holly and James down the driveway.

It felt very strange to walk into the DeCarrio's house when Katalie wasn't there. "The TV is upstairs," Holly said. "Katalie lets us watch it when she's not home."

Gretchen followed them both upstairs. "At the landing,

Holly gave her son a hug. "Remember to mind Mrs. O'Malley, now." With that she went back downstairs, and Gretchen heard the front door open and close.

Gretchen smiled at the boy. He was about five years old with curly black hair almost down to his shoulders and big brown eyes. "Well, James, what would you like to do?"

He looked up at her. "Mommy told me to watch real TV," he said.

"What is 'real TV'?"

The boy picked up the remote control, and at the click of a button a picture appeared on the TV screen. Gretchen gasped. It was their neighborhood! Right there on the screen was a clear view of the Stanley's house, with two people standing in the garage.

"James, is this the 'real TV' you were talking about?"

"Yeah. It shows what happened last week. Look, there's me on my bike, and there's Mommy. And there's the killers in that garage."

"Killers?" Gretchen narrowed her eyes. "Who told you

that?"

"Mommy did," the boy replied. Gretchen peered at the TV screen, noticing the dark shadows in the Stanley's garage. Suddenly she saw someone running between the houses, heading straight for the garage. The person was thin, wearing all black and carrying something long and thin.

The front door slammed and Katalie appeared. "What are you doing here?" she demanded.

"I'm looking after James while Holly goes down to the police station."

Katalie snatched the remote control out of the boy's hand and clicked it off. "James, you know I don't let you watch my TV." Then she turned to Gretchen. "I have this covered, Gretchen. You can go now."

James started to cry. "No, don't go! Don't leave me with her."

An odd feeling tightened Gretchen's chest. She couldn't quite put her finger on it, but she decided to trust her instincts. "Katalie, I really don't mind watching James until Holly gets back."

Katalie flipped her long blonde hair and fiddled with the gold bracelet on her arm. "Don't be silly, Gretchen. I do this all the time, believe me."

James sent her a look she couldn't fathom, part pleading and part something else. *He doesn't want me to leave.*

There was something wrong here. She didn't know what it was, but she sensed that something wasn't quite right. "I'll just stay until Holly gets back," she announced.

Without a word, Katalie walked to the TV, snatched the video out of the DVD machine, and disappeared down the hall. James pointed toward the hallway. "Mommy said she was the one holding the gun."

"Gretchen stared at him. "Gun? What gun?"

"The gun that person on the TV was carrying. I bet it was a rifle."

She thought about explaining to James that Larry had died of a heart attack, not from a gunshot, then decided against it. This whole tragic incident was getting blown way out of proportion.

But that night she couldn't get the image of that dark figure carrying something that looked like a rifle out of her mind.

Chapter Seventeen

# Oh, No!

Gretchen had spent the afternoon downstairs hanging family photographs when the phone rang. She picked it up to hear a man's voice asking for Jarrod. "I think it's Reilly," she whispered as she handed him the receiver. She listened to her husband's end of the conversation long enough to become uneasy.

"No hunting!" she mouthed.

He swatted her away with his free hand and continued talking. After a few minutes he hung up. "Reilly is upset," he explained. "He says he needs to talk to some of the guys."

"You're not going hunting are you?"

Jarrod patted her shoulder. "It would be just him and Gian Carlo. Maybe Darrell Levine. I forget exactly."

She sighed. "Jarrod, I don't think this is a good idea."

"Come on, honey, what could happen?"

"Jarrod, there are two lawsuits pending in the neighborhood, and one of them is directly related to Reilly. We already know about Reilly's history, and he's accused of shooting Chet."

"Gretchen, he's innocent until proven guilty, right?"

She sighed. "Where are you going?"

"To the wetlands about an hour north of here. We're going duck hunting."

She sniffed. Duck hunting! *What is it with men that they have to shoot things?*

That evening Jarrod got out a pair of boots and some warm socks, but when Gretchen walked into the bedroom he was standing with his hand on his chin. "I don't have any hunting gear."

"What is 'hunting gear'?"

"Oh, you know, honey. Warm things."

She pressed her lips into a thin line and went to bed, feeling in her bones that this hunting trip was a bad idea.

At four in the morning, Jarrod rolled out of bed, got dressed, and walked to the front door. Gretchen got up, cinched her pink robe tight about her waist, and studied him. He wore khaki pants, a plaid wool shirt, and a black wool jacket. She stopped him at the door.

"Call me when you head home."

"Sure. 'Bye, honey. Try not to worry."

Was he kidding? Jarrod had never been hunting in his life!

"You're kidding, right?" She peeked out the front window to see Darrell walking toward Reilly's house. Then, out of the corner of her eye she saw Holly Winston, dressed in camouflage gear standing next to Reilly's car. *That's odd.* Jarrod hadn't mentioned that Holly was going hunting, too. The question was *why*.

All right, she wouldn't worry. She went back to bed and tried to go back to sleep, but something kept nagging at her. Finally she threw off the comforter and stumbled to the den to watch TV. At this hour there wasn't much on, so she pressed the play button on their security system recording.

The screen showed the neighborhood in detail, even Mr. Parker eating something at the far end of their yard. Suddenly Gladys appeared, wearing her hat and boots, with her binoculars around her neck and holding a clipboard. A moment later Maggie showed up. She seemed upset. Gretchen looked more closely. Why, she was crying!

Gladys went over, said something to her, and patted her shoulder. Gretchen fast forwarded to see Darrell and Marie walking toward Sir Richard Road, and then Gladys appeared again, spoke with them, and wrote something on her clipboard.

*Wow, Gladys sure gets around. Why doesn't she just watch the goings on in the neighborhood on her own security system?*

She switched off the TV and leaned her head back against the sofa cushion.

Some time later, she woke to hear Mr. Parker barking. When she looked out the living room window, she spied the Stanley boys working in their front yard using a leaf blower and a loud lawn mower. And oh, my heavens, there was Gladys again, standing on her deck in her pajamas and an overcoat with her binoculars hanging around her neck. *That woman watches everything!*

Gladys saw her and waved, but Gretchen decided to ignore

her. Just as she turned away from the window Mr. Parker started vomiting on the kitchen floor. She grabbed paper towels, but as she was mopping up the mess the dog plopped onto the floor at her feet and didn't move. Gretchen dropped the towels and bent over him.

"Mr. Parker!" No response. Oh, God, something was wrong. She scooped him up, grabbed her purse, and raced down to her car. She laid him on the passenger seat and frantically fumbled in her purse for her car keys and the cell phone.

Before the electric garage door opener had completely raised the door, she backed the car up, then heard the bumper crash into the wood. She jammed the car back in drive, moved forward a few inches, and while the door was opening fully she managed to dial the vet. Then she slammed the car into reverse. The tires squealed as she roared out onto the street.

All the way to the vet's office she bit her lip at every stop sign and reached over to comfort Mr. Parker. Finally, *finally*, she pulled up at the Shellville Veterinarian Hospital on Drake Boulevard, gathered the limp animal in her arms, and stumbled to the entrance.

A technician in blue scrubs met her at the door. "I'll take him." He disappeared through a doorway.

"We saw you drive up," the young woman receptionist said. "Wait right here."

Gretchen started to cry, and the receptionist pressed a cup of water into her hand. She couldn't concentrate on the paperwork the woman handed her, so she paced back and forth and watched the big clock on the wall. After what seemed like hours, a tall man with white hair and a mustache opened the inner door.

"Mrs. O'Malley, I'm Dr. Francis. I'm afraid your dog has been poisoned."

"What? Poisoned? How could that be?"

"It appears he has ingested agapanthus bulbs. They're highly poisonous." He shook his head. "He's in kidney failure."

"Oh, my God! Will he . . . will he die?"

Dr. Francis touched her arm. "Do you have any idea where he may have gotten those bulbs?"

"No. We just moved into a new neighborhood, and there are

no agapanthus growing in my garden. I have no idea . . ."

"It's not the plant that's poisonous, Mrs. O'Malley. It's only the bulb."

Gretchen looked up at him through eyes blurred with tears. "What does this mean?"

The doctor pointed to a door off the reception area, opened it, and escorted her to a chair in the small room. "It means you have a decision to make. We could send him to the hospital in Naxton, where he could be put on life support. Or you could decide to do the humane thing and have him put down now. I have to warn you that he will not recover."

She sank onto a hard-backed straight chair, and the doctor sat down next to her. "The poison has permeated his entire system, Mrs. O'Malley. His organs are failing."

"Oh," she said in a shaky voice. "Can I see him?"

"Of course." He touched her shoulder. "I'm so sorry to have to say this, but at this point the humane thing to do would be . . ." She stood up, and he walked her to a small room at the back of the clinic where Mr. Parker lay on a steel examination table, hooked up to an IV.

*This can't be happening.*

"Oh, Parker," she choked out. The dog drew in a shallow breath as if to signal Gretchen that he knew she was there, and she laid her hand on his head. "You've been such a good boy," she whispered. "Such a joy for our family."

The dog opened his eyes and looked up at her. "Oh, Parker, we . . . we love you and . . ." Her voice broke. When she looked up, the doctor had tears in his eyes. Gretchen couldn't stop touching her beloved pet, and then she nodded. "All right," she breathed.

"I'll get the injection," the doctor said quietly. "First I'll give him just enough to put him to sleep, Mrs. O'Malley. He won't be in any pain at all."

Numb, Gretchen drew in a shaky breath and closed her eyes.

\*   \*   \*

She drove home in a daze, still sobbing. When she reached the house, she drove in, closed the garage door, and stumbled upstairs into the kitchen. The house seemed dreadfully quiet.

She walked straight to the bedroom, got into her pajamas, and crawled into bed.

Hours later, Jarrod returned from his hunting trip. "Honey?" He walked into the bedroom to find Gretchen curled up under the quilt. "Aren't you feeling well?"

"Oh, Jarrod," she wept. "Something awful has happened."

"What, honey? Tell me."

"I— I had to put Mr. Parker to sleep."

"Why? What happened?"

She rolled over and sat up. "He was poisoned."

"Poisoned! By what?"

"Agapanthus bulbs," she sobbed. "Lily of the Nile."

Jarrod sat down on the edge of the bed and pulled her into his arms. "Is that in our garden?"

She shook her head.

"Well, where would he get those bulbs?"

"Somewhere between Maggie and Katalie's house. It's on our surveillance camera tape."

"Do either Maggie or Katalie grow this lily thing?"

"I don't know. I don't think so."

"Honey, we need to tell the neighbors about this. Warn them."

"Now? Could you just call them?"

"No," he said. "We should go in person." He stood up and moved toward the door.

Gretchen tied her bathrobe around her and had just bent to put on her shoes when she noticed that Jarrod was limping badly. "Jarrod, what's wrong with your leg? You're limping."

"I'll tell you later," he said.

"What?" She planted herself in front of him. "Jarrod, tell me what has happened."

Chapter Eighteen

# **Neighborhood Watch**

"Jarrod, answer me. Why are you limping?"

"Okay, okay. Uh . . . it's nothing important, Gretchen. I . . . um . . . got shot."

"Shot!"

"Now don't get all upset, honey. The bullet just grazed my little toe."

She propped both hands on her hips. "Who shot you?"

"Um . . . well, it was Reilly."

"Reilly shot you? On purpose?"

"Oh, no, honey. I was just standing in the wrong place."

"Says who?" she demanded.

"Well, um . . . Reilly. He had his gun pointed down at the ground, and I guess I moved too close to him and he must have accidentally pulled the trigger."

She turned away without a word. Limping badly, Jarrod walked downstairs beside a furious Gretchen, out the front door, and over to the area between their house and the far edge of Maggie's yard. She looked up to see Gladys watching them from her porch.

Gretchen stopped. "I saw Mr. Parker out the window, eating something right over there."

She pointed. "See? The bulbs are still there! Jarrod, do you think Maggie knows about this?"

"I don't know."

At that moment Maggie walked out her back door. Gretchen stared at her, then noticed she was crying. "Maggie?" She pointed to the agapanthus bulbs. "Are these yours?"

"No!" Maggie sniffled."

Gretchen stepped closer. "What's wrong, Maggie?"

"M-my dog just died."

"Oh, my God. Do you know why? I had to have Mr. Parker put down today. He was poisoned by some of those bulbs. That's Lily of the Nile."

They stared at each other. "They're not mine, Gretchen. Honestly."

Jarrod moved forward. "Listen, Maggie. There are other animals in the neighborhood. And children. We need to protect them."

Maggie stared at the bulbs lying on her lawn. "I don't plant bulbs. I have no idea where those came from."

Gretchen sucked in a breath. "Then who?"

"I bet it's those Stanley boys," Maggie said in an unsteady voice.

Wordlessly, they looked at each other. Then for some reason Gretchen thought about Gladys. Gladys watched everything that went on in the neighborhood; maybe she'd seen something. She looked up, expecting to see the older woman with her binoculars, peering down at them in Maggie's yard.

But she wasn't there.

\*　\*　\*

"Honey," Jarrod said the following night. "There's a neighborhood watch meeting tonight at the Stanley's house. I found a flyer when I went out to get the paper."

Gretchen raised her eyebrows at him where he sat in his favorite recliner. One bare foot was propped on a cushion. He rustled his newspaper. "Hope they have plenty of chairs, because my toe still hurts."

She sighed. The last thing she felt like doing was attend a meeting, especially tonight. Her head still ached from her morning crying jag over Mr. Parker.

"Maybe they'll talk about the dog poisonings in the neighborhood," Jarrod added, watching her face. Gretchen said nothing. Maybe they would. It wouldn't ease the ache in her heart, but it might save someone else's pet. She studied her husband's elevated foot. "What time?"

"Five o'clock."

She put her chicken casserole in the oven, turned it to low, pulled on her heavy wool coat, and walked over to the Stanley's garage with Jarrod hobbling beside her. He'd managed to get both shoes on, but he was still limping.

The neighbors were gathered in the garage, and two police

officers stood in front of the small gathering, waiting for everyone to arrive. Dorothy and Reilly walked across the street and stood at the edge of the group. Gretchen had a hard time looking at Reilly. Jarrod, on the other hand, limped over to shake his hand.

"How's that toe, Jarrod?" Reilly inquired. They both looked down at his foot.

"It's fine," Jarrod said quickly.

Gretchen bit the inside of her cheek. Fine? Really? The man shoots my husband and he's acting like nothing happened? *It's fine, my foot!*

One officer, a tall, thin man wearing glasses and a crisp uniform, directed them to folding chairs. Behind him another policemen, shorter and a bit stout, looked out over the crowd and picked up a microphone.

Dana Sabbin tapped Gretchen's shoulder. "Sorry to hear about your dog, Gretchen."

"Maggie's dog, too," she murmured.

"Really?" Dana's voice rose. "Oh, how awful. I wonder

why?"

"Maggie and I think they were poisoned. Maybe accidentally."

"Or maybe not," Dana whispered. "What did the police say?"

"I didn't call the police."

Dana frowned. "You didn't? But someone did. If you didn't, then who did?"

Gretchen leaned toward Maggie, standing on the other side of her. "Did you call the police about your dog?"

"No, I didn't. I was too upset."

The older police officer tapped his mike for attention. "Folks, if I could have your attention?"

The crowd quieted.

"We're pleased to see you all here. Because of a recent unfortunate incident in your neighborhood, the Shellville Police Department decided to hold this meeting and tie up some loose ends. We'd also like to encourage you to set up a neighborhood watch as a way to stay safe and protect your families."

Gretchen noticed Lucille Stanley and the three Stanley boys standing off to one side. Maggie leaned toward her. "I wonder which one of those boys shot Larry Stanley?" she murmured.

"Maybe none of them," Gretchen whispered. "Otherwise one of them would be in jail."

Maggie stared at her. "Hah! I— "

The policeman cut her off. "Folks, the first order of business this evening is to remind all of you to keep any firearms under lock and key, preferably in a gun safe."

A man's voice rang out from the back. "What about Larry Stanley's murder?"

"Yeah," Chet Gaines shouted. "One of those young punks standing over there shot him. The gun was right there in the garage."

"Sir," the officer said, "Mr. Stanley's death is the first item on tonight's agenda."

"About time," Chet grumbled.

The policeman held up his hand. "Based on the autopsy report, no charges are warranted in Mr. Stanley's death.

Lawrence Stanley died of cardiac arrest."

Gretchen heard a collective gasp. So Lucille Stanley had been telling the truth. She caught Maggie's eye. "What a relief for the neighborhood."

"What about our dogs?" Maggie shouted. "Someone poisoned two of our dogs!"

"I guess *that* was one of the Stanley boys," Marie muttered. "My dog's been really sick. Those Stanley boys ought to be put in jail."

The policemen conferred with each other, but Gretchen couldn't hear what was said. After a long pause the slim man stepped forward. "We are aware of the dog poisoning incidents, and we are investigating them."

"I wonder who called the police?" Marie said under her breath. Gretchen shrugged.

"That brings up the main reason Officer Gordon and I are here tonight, folks. To keep your neighborhood safe. We'd like you all to set up a telephone hotline among yourselves." He produced a clipboard and handed it to Maggie. "If you would all sign your names and add your telephone numbers, we'll compile a master list for your convenience."

"Good idea," Jarrod said. Then he leaned to whisper in Gretchen's ear. "Don't add our new unlisted cell phone numbers. The last thing I need while I'm at work is a phone call from one of our neighbors."

Gretchen glanced up to see Gladys standing off to one side, her binoculars hanging around her neck, scribbling on her clipboard. *That woman sure writes a lot.* Every time someone approached her, Gladys clutched her clipboard close to her chest. A pen stuck halfway out of her scraggly grey bun.

Officer Gordon tapped the microphone again. "Everyone in this neighborhood needs to pay attention to things going on around them. If you see something out of the ordinary, call the proper authorities and then give your neighbors a heads up."

"What about that rifle in the Stanley's garage?" Darrell Levine yelled.

Tad Sabbin walked up, wearing shorts and a long-sleeved shirt and sandals, a frown on his face. He sidled up to Dana and smacked a kiss on her cheek. "What about the dogs?" he shouted, pointing his forefinger at the boys.

"Are our pets safe?" someone added. "And what about that rifle?"

"We have identified the owner of the rifle, folks. It's now being stored safely."

"Whose gun was it?" Tad pursued. Gretchen noticed Reilly and Dorothy standing at the back, staring at Tad.

The question went unanswered.

"The last person I want having my phone number is Lucille Stanley and those three boys of hers," a voice called out.

Lucille looked stricken, but the police officer continued. "Folks, I already explained about Mr. Stanley's death. We need to move on. Keep circulating that clipboard with your phone numbers."

"A lotta good that's gonna do," Marie Levine muttered. "I barely even speak to the neighbors."

"What?" Maggie blurted. "What about all our friendly block parties?"

"Marie, if you don't want to be included on the phone list, then don't sign it," Gretchen snapped. She felt like screaming at everyone tonight. At that moment there was a stir at the back of the crowd, and she turned to see the young woman who lived with the DeCarrios, laboriously crossing the street on crutches.

She stepped over to meet her. "Holly? What happened to you?"

"Oh, Mrs. O'Malley, I, um, tripped and fell into a ravine."

"On the hunting trip with Reilly and my husband?"

"Uh, yes." She looked down at the sidewalk.

Gretchen folded her arms. "It seems like people who go hunting with Reilly have a lot of accidents."

Holly's face twisted. "Maybe."

"Is your leg broken?"

"Um ... not exactly." The young woman shifted her crutches closer and scanned the crowd. "Actually, Mrs. O'Malley, I was hurt trying to get away from Mr. Hogan."

"Reilly Hogan? How do you mean, 'get away from him'? Why?"

Holly looked away and again studied the sidewalk. "It took about half an hour to get me out of that ravine. I pulled a tendon."

Gretchen peered more closely at the young woman. "Why?" she repeated.

Holly looked up, her cheeks scarlet. "Well . . . uh . . . he was trying to, um, kiss me, and I tripped and . . ." She looked over at the crowd of neighbors. "You won't tell his wife, will you?"

Gretchen bit her lip. Tell Dorothy? No, of course she wouldn't. But she'd sure like to tell Reilly a thing or two. Why hadn't Jarrod told her that part, about Reilly trying to kiss the girl? She glared at her husband, then turned her attention back to Holly, helped her over the curb, and walked with her to join the crowd.

The older police officer was speaking. "It's important for all of you to keep in touch with your neighbors, especially when unexpected things happen. We will make sure all of you have a copy of this master telephone list."

For the rest of the neighborhood watch meeting, Gretchen

tried to decide whether she was going nuts or this neighborhood was just plain crazy. Then Maggie got up to make an announcement.

"We have a new family moving in next week! Eli and Lisa Fontaine have bought the place across the street from the O'Malleys. They have two children, a boy five years old and a baby girl about twelve months."

Leave it to Maggie to know everything about everybody, Gretchen thought. But she was surprised at her reaction to the announcement about new neighbors. "I hope they won't be sorry," she whispered to Jarrod. "They might not want to move into this neighborhood if they knew all the crazy things that go on here."

Jarrod caught her hand. "Shh, honey! Maybe all neighborhoods are a little odd."

Gretchen gritted her teeth, then noticed that Gladys was still scribbling away on her clipboard, and now she was smiling. Does that woman ever stop writing? While the police wrapped up the meeting and collected the clipboard with all their phone numbers, she studied Gladys where she stood on the sidelines.

*There is something strange going on with that woman! I just can't put my finger on it.*

## Chapter Nineteen

## What Did She Say?

"Honey, do you hear that noise? What is that?"

Jarrod rolled over in bed and opened his eyes. "Sounds like a big truck."

Gretchen put on her robe and went to the front window where she had a bird's eye view of the entire street. A United Freight moving van and two smaller trucks were parked in front of the house next to the Stanley's. "Oh, it must be the new neighbors!"

She opened the blinds all the way to see Gladys on her porch, binoculars around her neck, writing away on her clipboard. Gladys waved, but Gretchen just stood there watching. *Wait until the new neighbors get a load of you, Mrs. Busybody!* She had just turned away to get the coffee mugs out of the cupboard when a smiling Jarrod walked into the kitchen.

"Good morning, honey!" He smacked a kiss on her forehead. "Did you figure out what the noise was?"

"A moving van. The new neighbors are moving in today. Maybe we should invite them over for supper tonight."

"Good idea. Moving is always tough."

"Why don't you make the coffee and I'll go downstairs and get the newspaper?" She cinched her robe tight, slid on the slippers she left by the front door, and headed for the driveway. Maggie's voice stopped her.

"I see you're not dressed yet!"

Gretchen winced. *Doesn't that woman ever sleep?* "Oh, good morning, Maggie." She smiled and started for the front door.

"Gretchen, wait! Guess what I found out about the new neighbors?"

"Tell me later, Maggie. I haven't time now."

"But— "

Gretchen escaped back into the house, and in the kitchen she slapped the newspaper down on the table and shook her head.

"Sometimes that Maggie really rubs me the wrong way. She's out there all dressed with her jewelry and high heels and everything, inspecting our new neighbors. I wouldn't be surprised if she'll be over there this morning, unpacking boxes for them."

Jarrod's eyebrows went up. "How about we ignore Maggie and her jewelry and go to the bakery for breakfast?"

Sometimes, Gretchen thought as she got dressed and followed Jarrod down to the garage, her husband had just the right idea at just the right time. "How's your toe this morning?" she asked when they reached the car.

"Getting better every day," he said with a grin. "Hardly limping at all now."

"Did you know Dana Sabbin asked if we were going to sue Reilly because you got shot?"

"Nah. What nut sues a neighbor because of a little accident?"

That started Gretchen thinking about the neighbors. Jarrod was right. What kind of neighbor *does* sue another neighbor for an accident? *I wonder if Dorothy and Reilly have settled their lawsuit with Chet and Maggie?* Then an unexpected thought popped into her head. Was Chet and Maggie's income really derived from lawsuits?

Strudel Bakery was a bustling wall-to-wall crowd of people. One table was free, near the window. Just as Gretchen sat down, two children at the next table started to fuss. "Mommy, Elise stole my crayon!"

The mother sighed. "Chris, finish your breakfast and stop pestering your sister." She looked up at Gretchen and smiled. She was a pretty blonde woman, dressed in slim black jeans and a cable-knit sweater. "The kids are a little out of sorts this morning. We're moving into our new house today, but all their toys are still packed."

"Oh?" Gretchen said. "You're new in the area? Where is your house?"

"Sir Richard Road," the woman said. "You know it?"

Gretchen nodded just as Jarrod sat down with two cups of coffee and a plate of doughnuts. "We live right across the street from you. Gretchen and Jarrod O'Malley." She reached across the table to shake the woman's hand.

"I'm Lisa Fontaine, and these are our children, Chris and Elise. My husband, Eli, is helping the movers unload our furniture."

"That's always really stressful," Gretchen said. "Maybe you'd all like to come over for supper tonight? I have some of our grandkids' toys and a high chair."

"That sounds nice," Lisa said. "Thank you so much!" Gretchen dug into her black purse, found a pen and a notepad, and scribbled down their phone number. "Call us when you're ready to eat."

"She seems nice," Jarrod said when Lisa and her children left.

"Yes, and not the least bit odd," Gretchen said. "What a relief!"

Jarrod chuckled, and while she dawdled over her coffee he ate all the doughnuts.

When they pulled into their driveway after breakfast, the

movers were busy carting boxes into the house across the street. Gretchen watched for a moment and then noticed something.

"Jarrod, look!"

He turned off the engine. "What?"

"Maggie is over there, standing right by that moving van, directing the movers! She's probably driving Lisa nuts."

"Yeah, probably. Let's go inside."

In the kitchen Gretchen got busy putting together a simple dinner of spaghetti and meatballs, and around five o'clock that afternoon, the doorbell rang. "Jarrod, could you answer that? I'm right in the middle of my green salad."

She heard him greet their dinner guests, and then he ushered them upstairs. "You must be Eli," she called. "How's moving day going?"

Eli sighed. He was tall and athletic-looking, with an unruly shock of dark brown hair straggling over his forehead. "I don't remember all this stuff when we were packing!" he said with a laugh.

"We have enough furniture for two houses," his wife added,

herding the children into the kitchen. The little girl was just barely walking.

"We really appreciate this," Eli said. "In fact, the whole neighborhood seems really helpful."

"A tall redhead, really dressed up like she was going to church, came by to unpack our boxes," Lisa said. "What with two kids running around and that woman diving into all my kitchen cartons . . ." Her voice trailed off. "Well, I finally had to shoo her out! It was just too much."

Gretchen bit her lip. "That would be Maggie Gaines, my next-door neighbor. She did the same thing when Jarrod and I moved in last year."

"I hope I didn't make her mad, but I like to organize my kitchen things in a certain way."

Eli lifted his daughter into the high chair. "Someone named Chet came over this afternoon while the movers were putting boxes in our garage." Jarrod and Gretchen looked at each other.

"He brought over a drill and some pegboard," Eli continued. "Said it was a neighborhood tradition that he find just the right spot for the pegboard and hang it up. I told him to get the hell out of my garage, and he left in a hurry."

Jarrod laughed. "Funny you mentioned that, Eli. Earlier today I fixed the pegboard that Chet hung up in *my* garage when we moved in. It was mounted crooked and had cracked the plaster, so I had to spackle the wall and repaint it."

"That's Chet Gaines," Gretchen explained. "He's married to Maggie."

"Oh, yeah?" Eli said. "Then who's the heavy guy named Rippy or something. He stopped by an hour ago, wants me to go hunting with him."

"That would be Reilly," Gretchen said. "Don't go hunting with him."

"Oh? How come?"

Jarrod cleared his throat. "Well, I went hunting with him recently, and it didn't turn out so well." Gretchen waited for him to explain about his toe, but he didn't mention it.

"Then an older guy with real black hair and bushy grey eyebrows stopped by with his wife. She gave us some jam she'd made."

"She seemed nice," Lisa added.

"That's Darrell and Marie Levine," Gretchen said. "They live at the end of the block, and yes, they're quite nice." *Even though Darrell is trying to recapture his youth at the beauty parlor.*

When supper was over, Eli, Jarrod, and the children moved into the living room while Lisa helped Gretchen clear the plates off the table. Suddenly Lisa yelped. "Gretchen!" She pointed out the kitchen window. "There's a woman staring at us from that house over there. Why, she has binoculars!"

"Honey?" Jarrod called from the other room. "Is everything okay in there?"

"Everything is fine. Lisa just met Gladys for the first time!"

She pressed her lips together. *How much should I tell our new neighbors about our very odd neighbors? It doesn't seem fair to not give them some warning.*

\*     \*     \*

The following morning, Gretchen and Jarrod were having

coffee in the kitchen before he left for work when Gretchen suddenly reached her hand to his forearm. "Jarrod, there's something bothering me, and I don't know what to do."

He set his cup down on the table. "Oh? Is it about Mr. Parker?"

"No, it's about the neighbors. The new ones."

Her husband raised his eyebrows and turned his head toward her. "They seem okay, honey. What's worrying you?"

She hesitated. "Do you think we should tell them about all the chaos in this neighborhood? You know, about Maggie and Chet's lawsuits and Holly getting hurt on that hunting trip, and Gladys and her binoculars, and— "

"No," he said shortly. He stood up and set his coffee cup in the sink. "Absolutely not. Don't stir up trouble, Gretchen. Who knows, maybe all the strange things that have happened since we moved in are just flukes."

She stared at him. "Oh, Jarrod, you don't really believe that."

"I don't?"

"No, you don't." She expelled a long breath. "Nothing has been a fluke since we moved in."

He hugged her and gave her a kiss on her cheek. "I need to get to work and leave you to mull this over. See you around six."

"Sure," she murmured. "Six. We're having chicken." When the front door closed behind him, she walked into the living room and pulled open the blinds. Across the street the new neighbor boy, Chris, was playing with a dog on his front lawn. Her heart raced. Pets weren't safe in this neighborhood, at least not until the agapanthus bulb poisonings were explained. She grabbed her jacket and raced down the stairs.

"Hi, Chris." She bent down to pet the animal, a cute little black terrier. "Is this your dog?"

"Hi!" he said excitedly. He looked at her with the most beautiful blue eyes. "It's mostly mine," he said with a grin. "Elise is too little to play with it, and Mommy said I'm a big boy now and I get to."

"What's his name?"

The boy grinned. "Chewy. Mommy says his name fits him."

The front door opened, and Lisa stepped out. "Chris, come inside. Leave Chewy outside."

Gretchen straightened up and waved. "Good morning, Lisa. How are you?"

"I'm fine," she said quickly. Chris scooted past her and disappeared inside.

But it was obvious Lisa wasn't fine. She was wearing faded jeans and an old tee-shirt, and her eyes looked tired. Her usually neat blonde pony tail was straggly. "Is everything okay?" Gretchen asked. "You look worn out."

Lisa glanced behind her. "Oh, gosh, is it that obvious? I'm worn out because . . ." She tipped her head toward the house. " . . . *she's back!*"

"Who's back?"

Lisa rolled her eyes and pointed behind her. "That woman, Maggie. She's in my kitchen, unpacking all my china."

Gretchen started to say something, but at that moment Maggie stepped out on the porch. She was all dressed up, as usual, in white slacks and high heels. "Hi, Gretchen. Did you come over to help? It's a real mess in here." Maggie turned around and went back upstairs. "So much to do, so little time!" she muttered.

Lisa frowned and moved closer to Gretchen. "How do I get rid of her?" she whispered. "She's driving me nuts!"

Gretchen nodded. "I can imagine," she said quietly. "Maggie's like that, really pushy. Listen, there's something you should know."

"Is it about Maggie?" she murmured.

"No. It's about your little dog. I think you should keep it inside, away from the neighbors."

Lisa frowned. "But why? That's really hard to do with a five-year-old."

"Well, the reason is because two dogs in the neighborhood have died in the past few weeks, mine and Maggie's. They were poisoned, apparently by eating Lily of the Nile bulbs. They're toxic for children, too."

"Oh, my God!"

"Maggie didn't warn you? She should have," Gretchen said

quietly.

"I wonder why she didn't?" Lisa glanced up.

"Maybe because she's distracting herself by unpacking your boxes!"

Lisa laughed, then caught her breath. "But that's awful! That's so selfish!"

Gretchen patted her shoulder. "Well, that's Maggie. I suggest you get tough, if you know what I mean."

"Oh, thank you, Gretchen. Yes, I know exactly what you mean. And thanks for the heads up about our dog."

She gave Lisa a smile and walked back across the street to make a fresh pot of coffee. She couldn't help wondering if she'd done the right thing, telling Lisa about the dog poisonings but not about the other things going on in the neighborhood. She peeked out the living room window and saw Lisa's front door open and Maggie emerge. She dashed across the street to Gretchen's front steps, and pounded on the door. When Gretchen let her in, Maggie looked furious.

"Do you know what Lisa Fontaine just said to me?"

"Why, no," Gretchen lied. *I have a pretty good idea, though.*

"Lisa told me to go home! She actually said she didn't want me in her kitchen!"

Privately, Gretchen sent congratulatory thoughts across the street to Lisa. And then she gritted her teeth and poured Maggie a cup of coffee.

Chapter Twenty

## Where Don't You See Her?

Just as Gretchen was backing out of her driveway to go to the hairdresser, she saw Holly hobbling along the sidewalk on her crutches. She stopped and rolled down the car window. "Holly, how are you?"

"Oh, I'm just fine," she said. Then she sighed and added, "No, I'm not fine, not really. My leg is a bigger problem than I thought."

"What's wrong?" Gretchen said. She felt so sorry for the young woman, having to limp around on crutches.

"It turns out the bone is fractured after all, just below the knee."

Gretchen winced. "Ouch!"

"I have to have surgery," Holly said in a subdued voice. "And I don't have any insurance."

"Why, that's terrible!"

Holly nodded and stared at the sidewalk. "Listen, Gretchen, I don't mean to be rude, but I have to get to a doctor's appointment, and my ride is waiting on the corner."

Gretchen watched the young woman lurch awkwardly on down the sidewalk, then noticed where she had come from. Reilly and Dorothy's house! As Holly was struggling into a blue sedan on the corner, Gretchen spied Gladys standing under her open garage door, scribbling on her clipboard. *I wonder if Gladys knows that Reilly made a pass at Holly on that hunting trip and caused her to break her leg?*

She decided to pretend she didn't see Gladys, but as she passed she glanced out the rearview mirror. Gladys was staring at her car and again writing on her clipboard. *What* was that woman doing?

For some reason finding a parking spot in front of Cut & Style was a challenge today. She watched all the people bustling around the stores and couldn't help wondering why so many were out shopping. *Was everyone shopping for Easter?* With a shrug she walked into the salon.

Toni was dressed in nice jeans, a black top that was cut out at each shoulder, and black, pointy high-heeled boots. Her hair was pulled up in her usual bun, but today she wore a big black sparkly bow on one side. "Gretchen! You're right on time."

Following Toni to the back station, Gretchen scanned the other customers to see if she knew anyone. She dreaded seeing Darrell Levine having his hair dyed. No Darrell, but she did recognize Sandra Livingston from the bookstore, who was just having her hair washed. Sandra didn't see her as she walked past.

"So," Toni said as she snapped the black drape around Gretchen's neck, "what's new?"

For a moment she couldn't answer. A lot had happened since she was in the last time; Mr. Parker's poisoning was still a sharp ache, and then there was Larry Stanley's death and Holly's hunting trip accident and the neighborhood watch meeting with the police and . . . Her mind felt overloaded.

"Well," she said finally, "I have new neighbors. A family of four. They moved in last week."

"Yes, I heard," Toni said. "Maggie came in yesterday. She sure doesn't like the wife, Lisa. Apparently she ordered Maggie out of her house!"

Gretchen stifled a smile, and Toni leaned closer. "Just between you and me, Gretchen, lots of weird things happen in your neighborhood, and they happen all the time." Carefully she parted Gretchen's hair.

Gretchen raised her eyebrows. *So it's not just me who notices how strange my neighbors are!* "Toni, if you lived in a crazy neighborhood like mine, how much would you tell your new neighbors about everything that goes on?"

The hairdresser looked thoughtful. "I think I'd let them find things out for themselves."

"My husband says the same thing."

Toni ran her fingers through Gretchen's hair. "I need to go mix up your hair color shade. I'll be right back." When she left, Gretchen bent down to pick up a magazine, "Shellville Today." She thumbed through the pages until a photograph caught her eye. *Why, that's Sandra Livingston!* She twisted to see if Sandra was still in the shop, then scanned the article. It was all about living in Shellville and the bookstore Sandra owned. She quickly read down to the last paragraph. *Ms. Livingston is currently working on a book.*

She remembered that Sandra mentioned once that she was writing a book. Now she wondered what kind of book it was.

Toni appeared, a plastic container of hair color in her hand. "Nice article about Sandra Livingston," she said, glancing down at the magazine in Gretchen's lap. "You know she's writing a book. I think it might be about Shellville."

*   *   *

When she left the hair salon that afternoon she decided to stop in at the bookstore. Just as she walked in, she saw her new neighbor, Lisa, talking to Sandra at the cash register.

"Gretchen!" Sandra exclaimed. "What brings you in today?"

"I'm looking for another book to read before I go to bed."

Lisa caught her eye. "Guess what, Gretchen? Sandra knows exactly where I live! I just love this little town where everybody knows everybody."

Gretchen drew in a long breath. *I sure hope you still like it after you spend a few months in our weird neighborhood.*

"There are some things that puzzle me, though," Lisa continued. "You know that woman with the binoculars?"

"Yes, Gladys. What about her?"

"Well, I saw the strangest thing today when I was walking our dog, Chewy."

Both Sandra and Gretchen looked at her expectantly. "What?" they said together.

"That woman, Gladys, was standing in *my* backyard with her binoculars focused on some boys in the yard next door."

"Oh? What was she watching?" Sandra asked.

Lisa turned toward her. "There was a tan car parked in front of our house. It's been there since yesterday, and she was looking at that."

"I saw that car, Lisa," Gretchen said. "I thought it was yours."

"Oh, no, it's not ours," Lisa said quickly. "We keep our car in the garage. I thought it might belong to the people next door."

Gretchen bit her lip. *Should I tell her about the Stanley boys? Maybe not. I can't accuse them of wrongdoing just because something looks suspicious.* "Lisa, if that car is still there two days from now, you might want to report it to the police."

"Okay, I'll do that." Lisa nodded and turned toward the door. "Oh, look! There's that woman I was talking about, the one with the binoculars!"

Sure enough, there was Gladys, peering at them from behind a white Subaru parked in front of the bookstore. "That's odd," Gretchen said. "That is Gladys, but I've never seen her outside of our neighborhood."

Lisa stared at her. "I have such a strange feeling about that woman," she said as she moved toward the door.

"We all do," Gretchen murmured. When she turned back to talk to Sandra at the cash register, the bookstore owner had disappeared.

*   *   *

That night while Gretchen was frying hamburgers for dinner the doorbell rang. When she went downstairs, Lisa was standing on the porch, out of breath and obviously upset about something.

"Gretchen, I just got home with the kids, and I was taking Chewy out of his crate when I noticed that the sliding glass door at the back of the house was wide open! I am positive I locked it before I left the house."

Gretchen's stomach tightened. "Was anything taken?"

The young woman shook her head. "Most of our things are still packed in boxes so I can't tell if anything is missing. It's just so unnerving!"

"Have you called the police?"

"Not yet. And that tan car is still parked in front of my house."

Gretchen spent some minutes calming her new neighbor down, and when Lisa left, she went back into the kitchen to finish supper. Within a few minutes Jarrod arrived home from work.

"I waved to Lisa when I drove up, but she walked right past

me without even looking up. She looked really upset."

"Apparently someone broke into their house. Whoever it was left their back sliding door open."

"Oh, poor kids. They just moved in, too."

"Jarrod, I almost told her about Maggie and the neighbors breaking into our house at Thanksgiving. Then I thought better of it—they were really just trying to do something nice for us. So I ended up not mentioning it."

"Yeah, why make Lisa nervous, right?"

"I also didn't tell her about the Stanley boys and that stolen car a few months ago."

Jarrod took in a deep breath and sat down at the kitchen table. "It's probably best to keep quiet. Let the Fontaines find out about the neighbors for themselves."

Gretchen frowned. "Oh, honey, I really like Lisa and Eli. I want to warn them about some of the strange things going on in our neighborhood, but I'm afraid it might be meddling. When is saying something a warning and when it is gossip?"

"Don't know," Jarrod answered. Gretchen started to flip the

hamburgers, and after a moment he got up and walked into the living room. She had just opened the refrigerator when she heard his voice.

"Honey, I think you should come on in here," he called.

"Why? I'm busy making dinner."

"Just come and look out the window. The police are across the street! And it looks like they have one of the Stanley boys in the back of the squad car."

Gretchen dropped her spatula and joined him at the living room window. "And there's Gladys again, standing in our yard!"

Jarrod looked where she was pointing. "What's *she* doing out there?"

"With her binoculars," Gretchen added under her breath. "You know, there's something really suspicious about that woman. Every time anything happens in this neighborhood, there's Gladys with those binoculars. Someone should report her to the police!"

"Maybe," Jarrod muttered. "And maybe not. Maybe we should let sleeping dogs lie."

Maybe her husband was right. *But Gladys still gives me the creeps.*

Chapter Twenty-one

## What Next?

Gretchen could scarcely believe the scene unfolding on the
street below. The police squad car sat with its lights flashing and
Leonard Stanley sitting in the back seat, while neighbors began
pouring out of their houses. Before she knew it, Jarrod left her
side and joined them. Maggie and Chet stood on the sidewalk
while Lisa and Eli Fontaine were talking to the police officer. At
that point, Gretchen decided to go downstairs and stand in their
driveway.

Darrell and Marie appeared. Gretchen noticed Darrell's hair
was no longer jet black but blond, and his once-dark eyebrows
were now light brown and bushy. *I like him better with dark hair,*
Gretchen thought. *He's too old to be blond. But that's the point,
isn't it, to look as young as possible?* The man looked so
ridiculous she felt sorry for him. She turned toward Maggie to

hide her smile.

At that moment Lucille Stanley appeared in her front yard. "Dammit, Leonard, what have you done now?"

Leonard began yelling from the back of the police car. "I didn't do anything, Mom!"

"Oh, right," she said in a skeptical voice. "You didn't do anything." She moved closer to the police car, and the officer turned toward her.

"Ma'am, don't talk to him. Please step away from the squad car."

Lucille ignored him. "I'm not bailing you out this time, Leonard," she shouted.

Lisa Fontaine gasped. "How many times have you bailed him out before?" she called.

Lucille just looked at her in silence. Then Gretchen noticed that Gladys was standing near the lilac bush in the Fontaine's front yard, writing on her clipboard. Lisa saw her, too.

"What are you doing over there?" Lisa yelled. She started toward her. "Stop that!"

The police officer intercepted her. "Ma'am, do you want to press charges?"

"Of course I do! For God's sake, he broke into our house. I found him upstairs, in our bedroom!"

"Then one of you will have to come down to the station."

"Officer, I think that woman over there with the clipboard saw something. Why don't you ask her?"

"Ma'am," the officer replied, "we have a trespassing suspect in custody and a stolen car in front of your house. Is that woman with the clipboard really the problem here?"

The neighbors all stared at Gladys, who immediately snatched up her binoculars and pretended not to notice.

"What about that car in front of my house?" Eli Fontaine asked.

"We'll check the registration and have it towed to impound, sir."

Eli caught Jarrod's eye. "Watch my house until I get back." Jarrod started to say something, but Maggie interrupted him. "Don't worry, Eli," she yelled. "All of us will be watching!"

Eli stared at her. Lucille Stanley put her hand on his arm and whispered something to him. Whatever it was, it made him frown, and he started moving toward his car just as Katalie DeCarrio walked up.

"What is happening? Is it one of the Stanley boys again?"

"Looks like it," Maggie said.

Lisa confronted her. "What is going on? You mean you all know something about those boys in our neighborhood?"

No one said a word, and Lisa turned to Gretchen. "Why didn't you warn me?"

Gretchen felt everyone looking at her. "I didn't know what to tell you," she said.

Lisa wasn't satisfied. "What does that woman over there with the binoculars have to do with all of this?" she said angrily. "Just what is she writing all the time?"

Gretchen and the other neighbors turned to look at Gladys, but she had disappeared. "We don't know what she's doing," Maggie said. "She just appears out of nowhere whenever something is happening."

"Should we be worried about her?" Lisa pursued, her voice tight.

Reilly stepped forward. "Worry about Gladys? Nah. She's just an old woman all alone with nothing better to do."

Gretchen raised an eyebrow. "Really? How do you know that?"

Reilly folded his arms. "She's got no family. She hasn't even got a dog or a cat, so I think we are her only entertainment."

Lisa blew out an exasperated breath. "Well, it feels invasive to have someone looking at you every time you turn around. It's really strange. Whatever it is she's doing, I wish she'd do it somewhere else!"

Gretchen looked away. *Wait until she finds out about the surveillance cameras all her neighbors have.*

When the squad car finally pulled away, followed by Eli's Volvo, the commotion died down, and Jarrod and Gretchen went back inside to finish dinner. "I feel bad about not telling Lisa about the Stanley boys," she said in a subdued tone. "I should have at least warned her."

"What good would that do, honey?" Jarrod said, taking a bite of his hamburger. "Nobody knows when those boys are just being normal boys and when they're up to something illegal. We all hope the last time will be just that, the last time, but you never know."

"Did you see the look on Lisa's face when she realized Gladys was watching her? I know that feeling, and it's awful."

"Wait until she finds out everyone in this neighborhood is watching everyone else," Jarrod said dryly.

"Oh, my gosh," Gretchen blurted. "I need to warn her about all those surveillance cameras."

"No, you don't, honey. I'd be careful about telling her too much about this neighborhood."

"You know, Jarrod, I hate living across the street from the Stanleys." She got up from the table to put her dishes in the sink and gave a little cry. "Oh, glory be, there's Gladys and her binoculars again, staring at me while I wash dishes. She's even waving!" She reached up and snapped the blinds closed. "There! Let her write *that* down on her clipboard."

Jarrod pushed his chair away and walked over to put his arms around her. "I didn't think you were this upset about all these neighborhood antics."

"Well, now you know." She laid her head on his shoulder. "You know, sometimes I wish we'd never moved into this neighborhood."

"Oh, honey, we just moved in here!"

"So? We can move out again, can't we?"

He groaned. "Tell me you're not serious."

She gave him a long look, then kissed his cheek. "Okay, I'm not serious."

*Yet.*

\*   \*   \*

Two mornings later Gretchen woke up the sound of a voice yelling somewhere outside. She pulled on her robe and looked out the front window to see Lisa Fontaine standing in the middle of the street, trying to pull Gladys's clipboard away from her. "Stop that!" Lisa shouted. "I said, stop it!"

Gladys said nothing, just hugged her clipboard close to her

chest. In the next moment she disappeared between Gretchen and Maggie's house, and Gretchen opened her front door.

"Lisa, is something wrong?"

"Gretchen, doesn't that woman ever stop spying on everyone?" She sounded exasperated, and she sped over to Gretchen and propped her hands on her hips. "It's that Gladys woman. What is she doing writing on that clipboard of hers all the time? It's really weird!"

Gretchen sighed. "Has something happened?"

"It most certainly has," Lisa snapped. "That woman showed up in front of my house while Eli and I were talking before he left for work, and it looked like she was writing down everything we said. Before that she was watching us through those stupid binoculars. What is her problem?"

"I don't know," Gretchen said. "Gladys is a mystery to me, too."

"She's nosy! She's invading my privacy!"

"I know, I know. She invades my privacy, too. She peers at me through my kitchen window. I've wondered what Gladys is up to ever since we moved in."

"I think we should do something about her," Lisa said in a confidential tone.

Gretchen folded her arms across her midriff. "Well, it is certainly annoying to have Gladys watching us all the time, but it isn't illegal."

"Maybe. Do you know anything about her?"

"No, I don't. Nobody talks about her much. Reilly Hogan says she has no family. He thinks Gladys gets some sort of kick out of watching her neighbors. Maybe she's just lonely."

Lisa frowned. "Oh, that's really sad. But she is so annoying, always peering at us. Maybe there is a reason why she does it."

"Maybe." Gretchen thought for a moment. "Maybe we should just ask her."

\*     \*     \*

Gretchen had just finished a second cup of coffee when Maggie appeared on her doorstep, wearing fashionable khaki slacks, a red silk blouse, and high heels. Gretchen gritted her teeth. *Does this woman ever relax and have a down day?*

Maggie's eyes dropped to Gretchen's bare feet. "I see you aren't dressed yet."

"No, I . . . something came up before breakfast." She expected Maggie to ask what it was; when she didn't, Gretchen hid her surprise.

"I've decided something," her neighbor announced with barely contained excitement. "I'm going to have a tea party."

"Oh?"

"It'll be a real English tea. Everybody will get all dressed up. We'll even wear hats!"

Gretchen sighed. "Ah. That will be nice." *Right now I feel like a tea party about as much as going on one of Reilly's hunting trips.*

"I have your invitation right here," Maggie said, waving a card at her. Gretchen accepted it, smiled, and slipped it into the pocket of her robe. When Maggie left, she got dressed and decided to go out to run errands.

Backing the car out of the driveway she spied Gladys with her binoculars hanging around her neck, perched on a stepladder apparently adjusting a light bulb over her garage door. Gretchen tightened her lips. She had half a mind to stop and confront the woman, then thought better of it. She'd need more coffee before tangling with Gladys.

Just as she turned into the mini-mall parking lot, she saw Marie Levine standing outside Strudel Bakery. She parked the car, got out, and walked toward her.

"Marie! Fancy seeing you here!"

Marie looked up and smiled. "I was supposed to meet a friend for coffee, but I guess she forgot. I really wanted to talk to her."

"I have a few minutes before I run my errands. Would you like to have coffee with me?"

Marie nodded, and they found an empty table at the back of the bakery. While they were ordering coffee, Gretchen noticed that Marie was frowning. "Marie? Is everything okay?"

Marie looked away, cleared her throat, then caught her eye. "It's Darrell. I think he's having a thing with that girl who lives across the street, Holly."

Gretchen choked on her coffee. "What? What on earth gave you that idea?"

Marie lifted her left wrist and flicked a switch on the tiny black screen of her watch. "Look at this video."

"You're filming your husband using your watch? I've never seen such a thing!"

"It's new. My son bought it for me. Darrell has a matching watch, but he doesn't know I have both our watches synched."

"Synched? What does that mean?"

"It means . . ." Marie lowered her voice. "It means I can watch everything Darrell does."

*Oh, that's outrageous! What next?*

"Darrell and Tad Sabbin meet up every morning to exercise together, and then they go to the beauty shop and talk to all the women!"

"Well, so? That's not so awful, is it?"

"Last week Holly was there, and she and Darrell made a date to meet later at the DeCarrio's house."

"Marie, that doesn't seem out of the ordinary. Holly lives

with the DeCarrios."

"There's more," Marie said. "Yesterday— "

At that moment Maggie sailed over, a cup of coffee in her hand. "Why, just look at you two sitting here! You look like you're talking about something really serious!"

Marie jerked upright and folded her hands in her lap. Gretchen just smiled and took a sip of her coffee. An awkward silence descended. Oblivious, Maggie settled into the chair across from Marie. "Did Gretchen tell you about my tea party?" She reached into her purse and took out a small white envelope. "Keep next Saturday free."

Marie stared at the invitation as Maggie rose. "Be sure and wear a hat, now!"

When she left, Marie leaned toward Gretchen. "Did you see?"

"See what?"

Maggie has a watch just like mine. I wonder if she recorded us?"

"Can she do that without our knowing?"

"Sure. Most people don't realize they're being taped."

"Isn't that against the law or something?" Gretchen asked.

"Oh, I don't think so. These devices are getting more and more technologically sophisticated. Pretty soon everyone will have one."

Gretchen stared at her. *Sophisticated! It's like something out of a spy movie!* Suddenly she didn't want to know any more about watches or Marie or Darrell or tea parties or anything. "I'm doing errands this morning," she announced, standing up. "I'm running late." Just as she left the bakery she saw Marie click a button on her watch. *Oh, my God, was she taping our conversation?*

The uneasy feeling in her stomach stayed with her all the way to the bookstore. Just inside the door she saw a small black surveillance camera with a notice beneath it. *You are under surveillance.*

Gretchen took a deep breath. She felt surrounded by eyes watching her.

## Chapter Twenty-two

## **The Tea Party**

For a while on the morning of Maggie's tea party Gretchen felt apprehensive. But as her usual Saturday morning edged into afternoon, she started to feel curious. There were subtle tensions between some of the ladies of the neighborhood; and some were not so subtle.

"Jarrod? Do you remember where we put that box marked Miscellaneous?" she asked her husband.

Jarrod rattled the sports section of the Saturday paper and chuckled. "We marked a lot of boxes Miscellaneous."

"It's not funny. Maggie asked us all to wear hats to her tea party this afternoon. I packed some of my mother's old hats away when we moved, and I want to wear one of them."

"You can borrow my baseball cap," he joked. He held it out to her.

"Oh, boy, Maggie would just love for me to wear a baseball cap! She was very insistent that this was to be a *proper* tea."

"Proper, huh? Sure doesn't sound like *this* neighborhood."

Well, no, it didn't, she admitted. Maggie suspected everyone of poisoning her dog. While Gretchen was equally puzzled about why Mr. Parker had died, she nursed her grief and waited for the mystery to resolve itself. Maybe the tea party was Maggie's way of flushing out the guilty party, if there was one. Then there was the disturbing suspicion Marie had shared with her, about Darrell and poor Holly, who was still on crutches. And Gladys, who was beginning to set everyone's nerves on edge with her ever-present clipboard and binoculars.

The afternoon should be interesting, so she'd better dig up some sort of a hat for the event. She sorted through the packing boxes she'd stored in her closet until she found one marked Mama's Hats. "I found it!" she called.

"Don't celebrate yet, honey. Gladys is walking up our front steps."

Gretchen opened the door, but before she could get a word

out, Gladys exploded. "Gretchen, have you heard the news?"

She took a step back from the older woman. "What news?"

"About Dorothy! She's left Reilly."

"What? How do you know that?"

"I met her as she was leaving her house, about six this morning. She said she was finished."

Gretchen glanced at the clock on the wall. It was only 8 a.m. "Finished? That could mean anything, Gladys. What makes you think— ?"

"It's true," Gladys insisted. "Dorothy said she couldn't stand to go through another lawsuit."

"Lawsuit! What does that mean?"

"I guess you haven't heard about Holly. She's suing Reilly. Dorothy told me you advised her to sue him. Because of her accident, you know."

"What? I did no such thing, Gladys. Why would she say that?"

"Well, I sure don't know," Gladys snapped. "Maybe you should talk to Holly."

As quickly as she had appeared, the woman was gone, leaving Gretchen staring after her.

"Why on earth would Gladys come all the way over here to tell me this?" she murmured.

She puzzled over the matter for the rest of the morning, but by mid-afternoon she put it out of her mind and dressed for Maggie's tea.

She chose a burgundy silk dress with an empire waist, and found the perfect pair of high heels in her closet. Carefully she pinned her hair in a neat bun at the nape of her neck and placed her mother's burgundy felt hat with a see-through veil on her head, then decided to wear her pearl earrings and her Seiko watch.

"Wow, look at you!" Jarrod exclaimed when she walked into the living room. "You look great, honey!"

She didn't feel great. She felt nervous for some reason. She shook off the feeling and left for Maggie's house.

Just as she rang the doorbell, she heard someone walk up behind her. "Hi, Gretchen," Lisa called. She wore a short-sleeved green knit dress that came just below her knees, and her blonde hair was loose. Gretchen had to laugh when she saw her hat.

"I bet your kids loved it when you put their Goofy ears on top of that little green top hat."

Lisa smiled. "This was the closest thing to a hat I could come up with."

The door opened, and Gretchen watched Maggie's face. "Lisa, you must have visited Disney World recently," she said dryly.

Gretchen stifled a laugh and focused her attention on the tiara perched on Maggie's head. *Wow, I haven't seen anyone wear a tiara for decades.*

"It's real," Maggie volunteered. "I have another one that my parents bought me for a wedding present so I could pass it down to a daughter some day."

"That's nice," Gretchen murmured. They followed Maggie into the dining room.

"Gladys is already upstairs with Dana," she whispered. "She wore that godawful furry hat of hers. And Dana," she went on in a disapproving tone, "arrived in sweatpants and a sun visor! Imagine, *for a tea party!*"

Lisa caught Gretchen's attention and rolled her eyes as the doorbell rang.

Dorothy appeared, wearing a pair of grey sweatpants and flipflops. A baseball cap barely covered her frizzy brown hair. "I'm sure you heard I had a bad morning today," she barked. She stomped past Maggie.

"What happened?" Maggie asked, but Dorothy was taking the stairs two at a time and didn't answer.

Marie arrived next, wearing a calf-length challis dress that rippled as she walked and matching blue shoes and purse. On her head was a stylish blue hat that curved up on one side of her head and had a heavy veil that covered her eyes. Maggie smiled at her, but it quickly faded when Holly limped up on her crutches, wearing a child's birthday hat. It was pointy, covered with big red and yellow circles, and held in place with a rubber band around her chin. "It was all I could think of to wear," Holly said as she laboriously climbed up the stairs.

Maggie just stared at her. And then Katalie arrived, also wearing a tiara.

Maggie's gasp was audible. Katalie's beautiful long blonde hair was done up on top of her head, and her tiara was the largest one Gretchen had ever seen. It was much more ornate than Maggie's, with a huge diamond sparkling smack dab in the center. Katalie beamed.

Marie leaned toward Gretchen. "She sure got Maggie's instructions about wearing hats," she whispered. Unable to think of anything to say, Gretchen just stared. But Marie wasn't finished.

"I see Holly is here," she muttered. "Little tramp."

"Marie!"

Maggie hurried over. "Now, what are you two whispering about? Something interesting?"

"Nothing I want to talk about right now," Marie said bluntly.

Maggie's eyebrows went up. "Oh, honey, did Darrell come home with another one of those awful hair dye jobs?"

Marie's eyes widened. Gretchen looked from her to Maggie

and back.

"Come on, Marie," Maggie coaxed. "You can tell me."

"It's none of your business," Marie said, her tone decisive.

*Oh, my Lord, what on earth is going on? This is such rude behavior.*

But Maggie whirled away and clapped her hands. "Okay, everyone find your seats. Place cards are on the table in the dining room." The guests milled about the elegant table set up at the far side of the room, looking for their names. In the center sat a beautiful silver tea service, surrounded by plates of small sandwiches with the crusts trimmed off and tiny frosted cupcakes.

"Look at this!" Katalie exclaimed. "Maggie, you must have been up all night making those sandwiches!"

"Ladies," Maggie announced, "today we are feasting on fresh albacore tuna caught the humane way, and thin-sliced roast beef from cows raised without antibiotics."

Gretchen found herself seated between Lisa and Holly. *Well, how awkward is this!*

"And," Maggie went on, "I made the sandwich bread from scratch yesterday. I also mixed up three flavors of the cupcake batter and baked them in mini-muffin tins, just like Martha Stewart!"

"Oh, brother," Holly breathed. She ignored Gretchen, leaned forward, and spoke to Lisa. "I love your hat, Lisa. I had one just like it years ago when I took a trip to Disney World in Florida."

Lisa grinned. "That's exactly where I got this for my son! Cute, isn't it?"

But Maggie wasn't to be silenced. Undeterred, she went on. "I sewed those linen napkins myself, and that silver tea service is a family heirloom that belonged to my great-great-grandmother."

Gretchen noticed Marie turning her arm sideways and clicking the same button she'd seen at the bakery. *Is she taping this tea party?* She looked away, then noticed something really odd. Katalie, Dana, and Holly all had versions of the same watch but with different colored bands. And all three women were sitting with their watches pointed toward Maggie, who was standing at the head of the table.

Maggie sat down and glanced at her guests. "Now, we're all friends, so why don't we share what's going on in our lives?"

Lisa leaned toward Gretchen. "Is she kidding?" she murmured. Gretchen glanced at her and raised her eyebrows.

"See!" Maggie crowed. "Look at Lisa and Gretchen. They're friendly. I want us all to be that way."

Dorothy coughed ostentatiously. "If you didn't sue so many of your neighbors, we might be more friendly."

"What?" Lisa whispered.

Maggie swallowed. Both she and Holly stared across the table at Dorothy.

Across the room, Gladys started to laugh. "Oh, nobody in their right mind would sue a fellow neighbor! Right, ladies?"

The silence was deafening. Gretchen decided she had to defuse the tension. Carefully she touched her burgundy hat. "This hat belonged to my mother," she announced. "She wore it in the twenties, when women wore dresses and hats. My mother actually wore those nylons with the seam down the back. Do any of you remember them?"

More silence. She looked across the table at Marie's unusual blue hat. "Marie, I'm sure you have a story about that striking hat, don't you?"

"Well, actually I do," Marie said with excitement. "This hat belonged to my great-aunt Tabitha. She lived in London in the twenties, and she wore it to Buckingham Palace when she was an employee of the royal family!"

"Oooh," everyone breathed. "Who was ruling then?"

"King George the Fifth."

"Oh, my, how wonderful!" Maggie gushed. "The King of England saw this very hat!"

Lisa picked up the ball. "I bought this silly hat at Disney World for my son, Chris. That was two years ago, and it was the first time I had flown in an airplane."

The women all smiled.

"What about your tiara, Maggie?" Lisa asked. "I bet there's a story there!"

Maggie beamed. "You know, my mother made me enter beauty pageants. In college I won a Junior Miss pageant, and when I was twenty-one I was a princess during Mardi Gras. That's when I had my first alcoholic drink. It was called a Hurricane. And later I entered the preliminary Miss Universe contest."

"Oh?" someone said.

"Yes. But you know that life involves living with a certain lifestyle, so I dropped out."

Dorothy folded her arms across her ribcage. "Did you sue people back then?" she said under her breath.

Lisa touched Gretchen's hand. "What is she talking about?"

"I'll explain later," Gretchen intoned.

At that moment Marie leaned forward and addressed Holly. "Holly, you do know who my husband is, don't you?"

"Why, of course I do," Holly replied. "He's the older gentleman who gets his hair dyed at my beauty shop."

Marie snapped her mouth shut and stared at the uneaten sandwich on her plate.

Puzzled, Lisa touched Gretchen's hand again. "What's going on in our neighborhood?" she whispered. "Who is suing who?"

"Later," Gretchen whispered.

But Lisa wasn't deterred. "And just look at Gladys!"

Everyone twisted to look at the other end of the table where Gladys was busy writing on her clipboard.

"Gladys, what are you writing about all the time?" Dorothy asked in a loud voice.

All Maggie's tea party guests stared in Gladys's direction. The woman smiled blandly, slipped the clipboard into her oversized purse, and secured the strap under her arm. Suddenly Gretchen realized that both Marie and Holly were taping the entire scene.

Gladys stood up suddenly. "I have to go now." As she moved toward the door, her purse swung forward, accidentally knocking Maggie's tiara off her head.

Maggie shrieked. "Now look what you've done!"

Dorothy laughed aloud. "Sue her!" she shouted.

Everyone started talking at once. In the middle of the confusion, Maggie recovered her tiara and calmly began filling teacups using her great-great-grandmother's silver tea service.

Gretchen knew she could never explain all this to Jarrod, so when she got home later that afternoon she didn't say a word, just marched straight to the liquor cabinet and poured herself a double shot of brandy.

Chapter Twenty-three

## Who's Suing Who?

The next morning Gretchen was downstairs in the laundry room putting a second load of Jarrod's shirts into the dryer when she heard the doorbell ring. She raced up the stairs to find an agitated Lisa on her doorstep.

"Lisa! How are you?"

"Not good," the young woman blurted. "I'm getting really concerned about what goes on in this neighborhood. This morning the kids and I went for a walk around the block and we ran into Holly, that girl who rents a room in the DeCarrio's house. She was still on her crutches, and she was coming from Dorothy Hogan's house."

"And?" Gretchen prodded.

Lisa sighed. "Well, I found out all kinds of stuff. Last year your next-door neighbors, Maggie and Chet Gaines, sued

Dorothy and Reilly because . . . Oh, it's so silly! Reilly shot Chet in the rear-end, and they were awarded money for pain and suffering. Actually," she added with a sniff, "the bullet just grazed Chet's pants, but they sued anyway."

"Yes, I know."

Lisa glared at her. "Why didn't you tell me?"

Gretchen bit her lip. "Well, it's really none of my business. I didn't say anything because I don't like telling tales or talking about things I really know nothing about."

"Well, did you know that Holly is suing Reilly Hogan for assaulting her when they went hunting?"

Gretchen hesitated. "Well, yes, I knew that's what happened. Holly told me she needs to have surgery on her leg, but she has no insurance. I didn't know she was actually going to sue him."

Lisa shook her head. "Eli and I can't keep up with all the chaos going on in this neighborhood. Those Stanley boys next door were worrisome, but it seems like everybody else is weird, too. Except you, of course."

Gretchen arched her eyebrows. "You know, I can't blame Holly for suing Reilly. He shouldn't have put his hands on her."

"Gretchen, guess what else I found out from Holly? It was her fault your dog was poisoned."

"What?"

"Well, not Holly exactly, but her son, James. He told Holly he dug those agapanthus bulbs out of the DeCarrio's garbage can, and the next day he was tossing them around when someone saw him."

"Who?"

"Gladys."

"Gladys!" Gretchen gasped. "You have to be kidding. Why didn't she stop the boy?"

Lisa shrugged. "Good question. But the upshot is that now Maggie is suing Holly for negligence."

"Oh, for heaven's sake. Holly is just a young single woman with a child. She doesn't have any money. What could Maggie hope to achieve?"

"A better question might be why Gladys didn't stop that kid

from digging in the garbage in the first place." Lisa tightened her lips. "And speaking of Gladys, there she is at the edge of your driveway."

Gretchen peered over Lisa's shoulder. *What in heaven's name?*

"That woman is driving me nuts!" Lisa spun away, and before Gretchen could stop her she was headed down the front steps.

"Gladys!" Lisa shouted. "What are you doing here?"

Gladys, her binoculars glued to her eyes, said nothing, just backed away. But the ever-present clipboard slipped from under her arm and landed on the lawn. Lisa made a dive for it. Instantly Gladys stomped on it, pinning it under her shoe.

"Give me that!" Lisa yelled. She tried to wrestle it from under the older woman's foot and got her hand kicked. "Ouch! My fingers!"

At that instant Lucille Stanley drove past in her beat-up blue Toyota, jammed on her brakes, and rolled down the driver's side window. "Should I call the police?" she called, eyeing Lisa on the ground.

Lisa stood up, red-faced. "N-no, we're fine, thanks." Lucille shrugged and drove into her garage. Gladys, however, seized the moment, snatched up her clipboard, and disappeared between Gretchen and Maggie's house.

"Do you know what that woman had written all over that clipboard of hers?" Lisa sputtered. "Dates and names and things written next to them. What do you think that means?"

"I haven't the faintest idea," Gretchen admitted. "But whatever it is, it's strange."

*Really strange*, she thought when Lisa had marched off down the street. She went back to the laundry room and Jarrod's shirts.

When Jarrod got home that night, Gretchen spent an hour telling him about her morning while he tried to read the sports section of the newspaper. Finally she gave up and talked him into taking her out for dinner at Maria's Kitchen.

\*    \*    \*

The following day Gretchen was driving to the market when

she came upon Gladys in the mini-mall parking lot, striding rapidly along with her head down. Gretchen slowed. *Now, I wonder where she's going in such a hurry?* She parked the car and watched.

Her binoculars hanging from her neck, Gladys sped into the bookstore with her trusty clipboard clutched in her hand. Gretchen was about to climb out and follow the woman when she saw Holly hobbling toward her on her crutches. And oh, my heavens, the girl was crying!

Quickly she opened her door and stepped out. "Holly, what's the matter?" She reached into her purse for a Kleenex.

"Oh, Mrs. O'Malley," the young woman sobbed. "It was just an accident, honestly. Just a terrible accident."

"What was an accident?"

Holly covered her face with her hands. "It was an a-accident about your dog dying."

A jolt of pain bit into Gretchen's heart. "Holly, what are you talking about?"

The girl drew in a shuddery breath. "M-my son James told

me s-something last night. He said he was playing with some flower bulbs, you know, the ones that poisoned your dog and Mrs. Gaines's dog. He said he found them in the garbage can and w-was kicking them around the lawn like a football, and then he forgot about them. He had no idea they were poisonous."

Gretchen was torn between her own pain and poor Holly's obvious distress. "Oh, Holly, I know it was just an accident. You must feel terrible about what happened." She patted the young woman's shoulder.

"I feel just awful about it, Mrs. O'Malley. But . . . but . . ."

Gretchen stiffened. "There's more? Tell me."

"Well, I just found out that Mrs. Gaines is going to s-sue me because of her dog, and . . ." Her voice broke. "I don't have any money. I'm trying to raise my son on my own, and I'm j-just barely making ends meet."

Gretchen sighed. "Oh, Holly, I am so sorry. I don't know how anyone could hold you responsible for an accidental thing like your son finding those bulbs. Maybe Mrs. Gaines's lawyer will advise her there wasn't any negligence involved. Maybe

. . ." Just then she caught sight of Gladys, coming out of the bookstore.

"Maybe what?" Holly said. "Oh, there's that strange woman with the binoculars. Does she ever go anywhere without them?"

Gretchen pressed her lips together. "Evidently not."

"She was the one who came and warned me the day James got into those bulbs," Holly said. "I bet she was watching James through those binoculars the whole time he was playing out in the yard."

"I'll bet you're right about that," Gretchen agreed. She was so annoyed she was afraid her tight voice might crack.

"Not only that," Holly said tearfully, "James said that lady showed him the trash can where the bulbs were in the first place. And she showed him how to play catch with them."

Gretchen stared at her. "What? Why in heaven's name would she do that? She couldn't possibly have known what would result. She probably just wanted . . . Oh, I don't know what she wanted. It makes no sense."

"Well, she's coming toward us, and I certainly don't want to talk to her. I just wanted to tell you how sorry I am about your dog, Mrs. O'Malley."

Gretchen studied the young woman's tear-stained face. "I know it was an accident, Holly. I can assure you that Jarrod and I won't be suing you. We don't do that kind of thing."

Holly reached out and grasped her hand. "Oh, thank you, Mrs. O'Malley. I knew you and your husband were good people." She turned away and made her way laboriously on through the parking lot while Gretchen watched Gladys scuttle off among the parked cars, her binoculars still swinging from her neck.

*That woman is not only a busybody, she is a real nuisance in a neighborhood that already has plenty of nuisances.*

Chapter Twenty-four

## Rev Up Your Engines

The next night over dinner, Gretchen told Jarrod about poor Holly being sued by Maggie. "She said something really interesting, too."

Jarrod looked up from his mashed potatoes. "Yes? What's that?"

"She said that we were good people."

He laughed. "As opposed to being bad people?"

"Well, yes, I suppose so. Sometimes I think this crazy neighborhood is full of bad people, Jarrod. Just think about— "

A blast of noise interrupted her words.

"What the heck?" Jarrod pushed his chair back and bolted into the living room. After a moment Gretchen heard his voice.

"Honey, you'd better come look at this."

Her stomach tightened. *Oh my God, what now?* "Just tell

me," she called. "I don't want to see it."

"You're not going to like it," he called. "Come and look!"

Reluctantly, she joined him at the window and peeked through the blinds. "What is it?" Then she saw what her husband was talking about. Twelve motorcycles were lined up in front of the Stanley's house, all revving their engines.

"Looks like a motorcycle gang," Jarrod said. "That guy on the front cycle is wearing a skull and crossbones on his jacket."

"They all are," Gretchen said in a flat voice. All three of the Stanley boys were wearing the same leather jackets, and now they were waving the group into their garage! She turned away from the window, walked back into the kitchen, and set her dinner plate in the sink. When she looked up, she caught a movement in her shadowed back yard.

*Not again!* Gladys was racing across the yard toward the front of the house. "Honey?" she called out to Jarrod.

"Yeah?"

"This neighborhood is getting weirder by the moment."

"Huh! You said that last night."

She was silent for a long moment. "I guess you don't want to know what I just saw," she said at last.

"No. Yes! What is it?" he called.

"Gladys. Again."

Silence from the living room until Jarrod's voice sliced into her brain. "Oh, wow, come look at this! Lucille Stanley just climbed on the back of one of those motorcycles. She's wearing leather pants and a leather jacket and black boots!"

Gretchen got there in time to see Lucille wrap her hands around the waist of a burly guy wearing a bandana and a leather jacket with a skull and crossbones on the back. The machine sputtered to life and headed toward Sir Richard Road. The last thing she saw was Lucille's long grey hair streaming behind her in the wind.

"Jarrod, do you see what I see?"

"Man," her husband breathed beside her, "this is like a bad movie."

"Look." She pointed to a lilac bush near their mailbox. "There's Gladys in our front yard, writing on that darn clipboard!"

"And . . ." Jarrod said with a chuckle, "she's laughing!"

"Jarrod," Gretchen sighed. "For heaven's sakes, what is *wrong* with that woman? This is so Not Funny."

"Yeah." Jarrod put his arm around her shoulder. "Some movie, huh? Makes you wonder what's next."

*       *       *

The next night was the same, a group of motorcycles revving their engines and their leather-jacketed riders whooping it up. As the noise increased, Gretchen peeked out the living room window blinds to see Lucille Stanley sitting on a parked motorcycle with high handlebars, a bottle of beer in her hand.

"Jarrod, put down your newspaper and come look at this!"

"Wow," her husband breathed when he joined her. "What is that woman thinking? And look—Maggie and that woman Gladys are hanging around next to our mailbox."

In the next instant Gretchen was out the front door, crouching behind her lilac bush.

"Sheesh!" Maggie exclaimed. "Gretchen, you scared me half

to death. Where did you come from?"

"From inside my house. Why are you two out here hiding behind my mailbox?"

Gladys said nothing, but Maggie turned sideways and frowned at her. "You have to be kidding. We have a motorcycle gang across the street! Why shouldn't I be here?"

Gladys nodded so vigorously her grey curls bobbed.

"I'm making sure that bunch of idiots doesn't do anything illegal," Maggie added. "So far they're just drinking and gunning their motors, but you never know."

Gretchen sighed. She didn't know who looked more ridiculous, Lucille Stanley drinking beer on the back of a motorcycle or Gladys with her furry hat and her binoculars and Maggie, who was all dressed up in black silky slacks, high heels, and a sheer red blouse, huddled there behind her lilac bush. She shook her head.

Suddenly she heard someone on her back deck, so she jerked upright and made a beeline for the backyard. "Dorothy! What are you doing up there?"

Dorothy shushed her, leaned down, and cupped her hands around her mouth. "I saw Gladys and Maggie in front of your house," she whispered. "Those motorcycle guys are Hell's Angels. They're having a party right here in our neighborhood; I think they call it a 'rumble'."

Gretchen climbed the steps to join Dorothy, and all at once she heard a rustling noise below. Both of them peered over the railing to see a shadowy figure. "Katalie!" Gretchen blurted. "What are you doing there?"

"I've been watching you," the young woman said. "And those motorcycle guys."

"And Lucille Stanley," Gretchen muttered under her breath.

"If they don't stop all that noise we should call the police."

"Exactly," Maggie said from below them. "We sh— " She broke off at the sound of an explosion.

"W-what was that?" Katalie whispered.

Gretchen and Dorothy scrambled off the deck and raced to the front yard. "Oh, my God, look!" Dorothy screeched. "The Stanley's garage is on fire!"

Gretchen snatched her cell phone from the pocket of her jeans and dialed 911. While the women waited for the fire truck, the motorcycles began roaring off down the street. Then they heard Lucille Stanley's hoarse voice.

"Goddammit, Leonard! What were you thinking? You don't put a propane tank in the garage and then light a cigarette!"

Maggie stepped up beside Gretchen. "I taped the whole thing," she said, tapping her wristwatch. Gladys focused her binoculars on the Stanley house just as sirens sounded a block away, and in the next minute two fire engines screamed to a stop in front of the burning garage. A police car with flashing red lights and an ambulance followed.

In minutes, streams of water obliterated the flames, and Lucille Stanley sat sobbing on the curb. A police officer walked over and knelt down to speak to her.

The four women and Jarrod watched from their front lawn, but no one said a word. By ten o'clock the commotion had died down, the fire trucks and other vehicles rolled off down the street, and Lucille Stanley disappeared inside her house. The entire neighborhood smelled of smoke and charred wood.

"Lucky no one was hurt," Gretchen remarked. She hugged Jarrod.

"She's lucky the fire didn't reach the house," Katalie said sharply. "I don't know about that family. They're all bad news, if you ask me."

"Lucille will have to rebuild her garage," Jarrod said. "It's a real eyesore."

"This whole neighborhood is an eyesore in a way," Gretchen remarked. "Not visually so much as . . ."

"Metaphorically?" Maggie suggested.

"Yes," Gretchen agreed.

"Exactly," Dorothy breathed.

Gladys patted her furry hat and started off down the sidewalk. "I've got to go right home," she murmured. "I forgot my clipboard."

Chapter Twenty-five

# The Birthday Party

Just when Gretchen thought the neighborhood was getting back to normal, she and Jarrod were invited to a surprise birthday party for Marie Levine. Holly wandered up onto their front porch on Sunday to tell them about it. "It's at the DeCarrio's. I'm playing co-hostess with Katalie," she said excitedly.

Gretchen hemmed and hawed for a week, and finally Jarrod talked her into it. "What could go wrong at somebody's birthday party?" he joked.

*In this neighborhood? Plenty.* But despite her misgivings, the next Saturday afternoon she got dressed up, and they started off. "Look," Jarrod said as they passed the Stanley's house.

"Their garage is repaired. That was sure quick. Looks like all they need to do now is repaint it."

When they got to Gian Carlo and Katalie's, Holly met them

at the door, which was decorated with red and yellow balloons and a big Happy Birthday sign. "Come on in! Drinks are in the dining room. Dorothy and Reilly are already here."

"Dorothy and Reilly?" Gretchen whispered to Jarrod. "Does that mean Dorothy didn't leave him after all?"

Jarrod just shrugged.

They stood around with cans of soda in their hands, making small talk with Katalie and Gian Carlo until Gretchen suddenly heard Holly and Dorothy having an argument in the kitchen. She peeked around the corner to see that Holly's face was red. "I'm not interested in your husband, Dorothy. Why would you think such a thing?"

"Well, what kind of woman invites herself along on an all-male hunting trip?" Dorothy said, her voice rising.

"I didn't invite myself! Reilly asked me if I wanted to come and see what hunting was all about. Now I wish I hadn't been so curious."

"Then would you care to tell me exactly how you broke whatever it is you broke? I heard you came on to Reilly and he–"

Gretchen noticed Reilly escaping to the living room, where the TV was going full blast. Jarrod followed him.

"Reilly!" Holly screeched. "I had nothing to do with your husband, Dorothy. Nothing at all." She lowered her voice. "He tried to kiss me, and when I shoved him away I slipped and fell."

"Oh, sure," Dorothy sneered.

"Well, it's true! I told you I'm not interested in your husband. I'm only twenty-four years old, and he's an old man!"

*Oh, dear. No woman wants her husband to be described as "old."* Gretchen peeked into the living room to see if Reilly was within earshot. Without another word, Holly plowed past Dorothy, who stood with her hands propped on her hips, and breezed into the kitchen.

Dorothy touched Gretchen's arm. "That little tart is trying to get us to pay for her leg injury," she said under her breath.

"Oh, I don't think— Oh, look, Marie's here!"

Sure enough, a dazed-looking Marie Levine was coming up the stairs. "Surprise!" everyone shouted. Marie, looking embarrassed, clung to Darrell's arm. Darrell looked at his wife adoringly, and Gretchen gritted her teeth. *What a play-actor that man is.* A week ago at the bakery Marie had confessed that Darrell was acting strangely. She thought he was making passes at Holly. Was that true or not? Could it all be in Darrell's *imagination*?

Well, the man dyed his hair in order to look younger; maybe he had other fantasies, too?

At that moment a grinning Lisa tapped her on the shoulder. "Earth to Gretchen," she murmured. "You look like you're a million miles away."

"What? Oh, hi, Lisa. No, I'm not miles away, I'm right here. How are you?"

"Bursting with news. Did you notice the Stanley's garage has been rebuilt?"

"Yes. It looks very nice."

"Well, guess what I overheard last night while the kids were playing out front? Lucille and the boys are planning a surprise for the neighborhood."

Gretchen frowned. "A surprise? What sort of surprise?"

"I couldn't hear too much, but it has something to do with their new garage."

A dart of apprehension poked into Gretchen's brain. "If it involves the Stanley boys maybe we should brace ourselves."

Lisa laughed. "I better go find Eli. Oh, look!" She tipped her head toward the living room. "Gladys is here."

Sure enough, there she was, clipboard and all. Gretchen watched her for a full minute, then looked away. Gladys was watching everyone, and she had the oddest smile on her face, half self-satisfied and half disapproving. *I wonder how that woman manages to just appear at the exact moment when something odd is happening?*

She turned away to find Maggie gliding across the room toward her. "Gretchen, fancy seeing you here." She smiled and leaned in to give her an ostentatious air kiss.

"I don't know why you're surprised, Maggie. Everybody was invited to Marie's surprise party. So, how are you?"

"Well, I've been better. I just learned why my dog died. Holly told me."

"Yes," Gretchen acknowledged. "It's really too bad, but knowing it was an accident is some comfort, isn't it?"

"I'm working on that one," Maggie whispered. "I'm still talking with my lawyer about this matter."

Gretchen's mouth dropped open.

The party swelled noisily around them, and eventually Maggie drifted off to find Chet. For the rest of the evening Gretchen found herself tuning everybody out. She was tired of all the little day-to-day annoyances that living in this neighborhood brought. She was tired of the gossip and the strained feelings and the misunderstandings. Most of all she was tired of being tired!

She found Jarrod, told him she felt a headache coming on, and left before the candles were lit on Marie's birthday cake. When she got home she kicked off her shoes and hung her silk dress in the closet; then she put on her robe and slippers and curled up with the book she'd bought months ago: "The Help."

Halfway through the last chapter, she released a long sigh. Even women living in the Deep South had annoying neighbors.

She guessed that was nothing new, but she was sure they had tried to cope with all their crazy neighbors the same way she was. She read until Jarrod came home, then went to bed.

When she woke up the next morning she drew in a deep breath of sweet, summery air and felt her spirits lift. Her good mood lasted all day Sunday and Monday, but on Tuesday morning it all went up in smoke when Jarrod stepped outside to pick up the morning paper.

"Gretchen!" he shouted. "Come look outside."

*Oh, no, what now?*

She flew to the window and stared at the Stanley's house across the street. "Oh, good heavens, it's bright green!" she exclaimed. "Their house is a really awful shade of green."

"That's the ugliest color I've ever seen," Jarrod breathed beside her.

"It's called chartreuse. Do you think maybe it could be just a primer coat?"

He shook his head. "Oh, my God, wait until the neighbors see this!"

But they didn't have to wait. Maggie's voice could be heard a block away.

"No!" she screamed. "They can't do that! No. No. *No!*"

"Oh, God," Gretchen muttered. "Now she'll be suing Lucille Stanley."

An hour later, Maggie appeared on their front porch. "We're raising money to repaint that house," she announced. "Reilly and Dorothy are putting in five hundred dollars. So are Marie and Darrell Levine. And Lisa and Eli, too. We have over three thousand dollars!" She paused for breath. "Are you two in?"

"Well, yes," Jarrod said slowly. "I guess we could throw in a couple hundred. Who's going to pick out the new color?"

"A better question might be who's going to talk to Lucille?" Gretchen asked quietly.

For a long minute no one said a word, and then Maggie stepped forward and clutched Gretchen's hand. "Could you talk to her, Gretchen? Please?"

Her heart dropped into her stomach. "No," she said. "It's none of our business what color Lucille Stanley wants to paint her house."

"Oh, but— " Maggie turned to Jarrod. "Gretchen could figure out how to say it in a nice way, don't you think?"

Jarrod put his arm around her shoulder. "What about it, honey?"

"No," she repeated, stepping away from Jarrod's grasp. "I don't care how much money you raise, Maggie. It's Lucille's house, not yours or mine or anyone else's."

"Why don't you wait a few days, Gretchen?" Maggie said. "Maybe you'll feel more neighborly later."

That did it. "I feel plenty neighborly, Maggie," she said, her voice tight. "But part of being a good neighbor means leaving other people alone. At least that's the way I was raised. You know, live and let live."

Jarrod reached out and squeezed her shoulder. "Maybe Lucille will take a good look at her house tomorrow and decide that's an awful color."

"Maybe," Maggie snapped.

*Maybe*, Gretchen prayed. But even if Maggie was furious

and Jarrod thought she was being pig-headed, this time she was

on Lucille's side.

Chapter Twenty-six

## The House Paint Bribe

In the middle of the night Gretchen woke up thinking about the Stanley's house. Had the neighbors heard that she had refused to talk to Lucille about the paint color? She thought about it for an hour, and then another hour. Finally, on an impulse she slipped out of bed, grabbed her robe, tiptoed to the living room window, and peeked between the blinds.

The neighborhood looked quiet, as normal as any other neighborhood, except for Lucille Stanley's house. This neighborhood was anything but normal and, Gretchen could plainly see, Lucille's house was still chartreuse.

"Honey? What are you doing up?" Jarrod stood in the hallway, rubbing his eyes.

"I—I'm just looking at the Stanley's house. I know I said we shouldn't interfere, but maybe I was wrong."

"You're not wrong. Besides, you already made up your mind," he said. "Come back to bed."

"Knowing our neighbors, someone has probably already approached Lucille."

"Approached?"

"You know, given Lucille the money the neighbors collected and talked to her about changing that paint color."

"Well," he murmured, "we can only hope." He walked her back to their bed, where she snuggled up to him and stared into the dark. She wondered if anyone else was lying awake thinking about all the crazy things going on.

The next morning Gretchen opened her front blinds and looked across the street. "Oh, God," she moaned. "It's still chartreuse."

"You expected it to change overnight?" Jarrod said from the kitchen doorway.

"Well, no. Just wishful thinking." At that moment she noticed someone crossing the street.

"Jarrod, look! Maggie is walking over to Lucille's house

carrying a basket. And wow, is she all dressed up!"

"I wonder what's in that basket?" he said from behind her. "Money, maybe?" He took another look out the window. "I bet Gladys is lurking somewhere nearby. I bet she'd know what Maggie's up to."

Gretchen scanned their front yard. Sure enough, there was Gladys, hunched down behind the lilac bush by their mailbox. Very quietly she opened the front door and stepped out.

"Hi, Gladys," she whispered.

The woman jumped. "Oh, Gretchen! You startled me."

Gretchen tucked her robe up off the ground and crouched behind her. "What have you found out?"

Gladys held her binoculars in her left hand and poked her other hand out of the bush. "I'm taping it." She looked down at her right wrist.

Gretchen stared at the watch on Gladys's arm. It was the same kind of watch some of the other women had worn at Maggie's tea party. Silently Gladys pointed across the street. "Maggie's got some beautiful linen things in that basket. And," she said in a hushed voice, "she also has all the neighbors' donated money. She's over talking to Lucille right now."

While they both stared across the street, someone else joined them. "Hi, you guys," Katalie whispered.

"Holy cow," Gretchen gasped. "You scared me!"

"Well, I had to be discreet," Katalie murmured. "Gretchen, you're wearing your robe!"

Gretchen looked at Katalie. "So are you."

Together, the three women looked over at Lisa and Eli's house. Lisa was standing in her front room window, watching the three of them huddled behind Gretchen's lilac bush.

*Oh, my gosh, this must look ridiculous.*

"All the neighbors are watching," Gladys said in a matter-of-fact tone. "Marie is over there behind her hydrangea bush."

"Well, what's happening?" Katalie whispered.

At that moment Maggie darted back across the street. She looked like she was crying.

Gretchen, Katalie, and Gladys all poked their heads up as Maggie reached the sidewalk, and she gave a yelp. "Oh! You scared the hell out of me!" She swiped tears from her cheeks. "Where did you all come from?"

The women looked at each other in silence.

"Well?" Gretchen asked finally. "What did Lucille say?"

Gladys immediately bent over her clipboard, pen in hand. When Gretchen frowned at her, she stopped writing and tucked the clipboard inside her sheepskin vest.

"She said she'd think about it," Maggie snuffled.

"Did she accept the money you raised?" Gretchen asked.

"Oh, yes, she took the money all right. She snatched that basket right out of my hand. All I wanted to do was show her the money, not give it to her yet. Not until the house is actually repainted."

"Did she say anything?" Katalie asked.

"She sure did. She thinks we're all being too nosy, and that the color of her house paint is none of our business. And . . ." Maggie blew her nose. "I brought her four hand-embroidered napkins and some homemade jam and fresh-baked rolls to show my good will. She didn't even thank me!"

Katalie stuffed her hands in the pockets of her robe. "But that's the ugliest color I've ever seen on a house."

Gladys smiled. "It kinda glows when the sun hits it."

Gretchen's eyes narrowed. "I'm sure glad *my* house isn't across the street from it."

Maggie started to cry again. "But *my* house *is* directly across the street from it. What if Lucille keeps the money but doesn't re-paint her house?"

Gretchen bit her lip. "Oh, I think Lucille will do the right thing."

*Do I really believe that?*

She escaped into her house, and a few minutes later was pouring a cup of badly needed coffee when she looked out the kitchen window to see Gladys standing on her back porch with Sandra Livingston, the bookstore owner, of all people. *Well, that's interesting. Sandra doesn't live in this neighborhood. What is she doing here?*

Gladys was pointing to her clipboard and flipping back some pages. Then they both hunched over whatever was written there and laughed. Gretchen clamped her mouth shut. *What are those two laughing about? What does that clipboard have to do with anything?*

Overcome by curiosity, she walked out to her back patio. "Hello, Sandra," she yelled.

Both Gladys and Sandra looked up and waved.

"What brings you out so early?" Gretchen called.

Sandra smiled and waved again. "Oh, nothing much. I'm just having coffee with my friend Gladys. I like to keep up with her."

"Ah," Gretchen said. She couldn't say why she didn't believe this, but she didn't.

"I-- I'm almost finished with my book, Gretchen. Remember I told you about it?"

"Yes, I remember." She turned to go back into the house when she heard Sandra say something obviously not meant for her ears.

"We have to be more careful, Gladys. Maybe we should meet somewhere else."

Gladys said something, but Gretchen couldn't hear what it was. Even so, she had an uneasy feeling about it. Her instincts told her something was going on between those two, but she was at a loss figuring out what it was.

That afternoon when she drove to the hairdresser's, she ran into Annie Blumme. Out of nowhere, the interior decorator blurted a question that stopped Gretchen cold. "What the heck is going on in your neighborhood?"

"What do you mean, Annie?"

"I heard that someone painted their house some godawful color and the neighbors are all up in arms."

"Well, yes," Gretchen admitted.

Annie shook her head. "Can someone actually *do* that in your neighborhood? Don't you have a . . .a homeowners code of some sort?"

Gretchen pressed her lips together. "It's really not up to the neighbors to dictate what color someone wants to paint their house."

"Oh. Sounds intriguing, Gretchen. Maybe I'll drive over and

see what it looks like."

On her way home, Gretchen noticed a McWilliams Brothers paint truck in front of Lucille Stanley's house. *Oh, good,* she breathed. *The problem about the chartreuse house is going away.*

Chapter Twenty-seven

## What Could Be Worse?

On Tuesday, Gretchen drove to the mini-mall and walked into Cut & Style.

"Gretchen!" Toni waved from the back of the salon. "You're right on time."

Gretchen glanced around the salon, and sure enough there was Darrell Levine, getting his hair washed. She couldn't help wondering if he'd had it colored again.

Toni walked her back to her station and spread a silky black drape over her sweater. "What's new with your neighbors?"

Gretchen pursed her lips. "Maybe you've already heard."

"Oh, you mean about someone painting their house a really ugly green color? Yes, Darrell Levine told us all about it."

*Well, news does travel at lightning speed in this town.*

"Why do you look so gloomy about it?" Toni asked. "She is

going to re-paint, right? I heard the neighbors contributed to a fund to pay for it."

"Well, yes. The house is being re-painted as we speak."

"That's good, isn't it?" Toni said with a smile. "Your neighbors will be happy."

"Maybe not," Gretchen said.

Toni stopped spreading color onto Gretchen's roots and held her gaze in the mirror. "Why not?"

"Oh, I don't know. In our neighborhood, you never know what's going to happen next!" Then she lowered her voice. "It's odd that Darrell comes to the same hair salon I do since he lives just down the street from me. He must know that I see him getting his hair colored."

"Yes," Toni said softly. "Today his hair is a weird reddish orange color. And wow, with his bangs cut like that he looks like Buster Brown."

"What is he thinking?" Gretchen whispered.

"He's *not* thinking. He's trying to look like a young stud, and it's sure not working."

Gretchen sighed and put Darrell Levine's attempt to recapture his youth out of her mind. She made small talk with Toni until her hair was blown dry, then left to return home.

When she turned the corner onto Sir Richard Road, her mouth dropped open and she jammed on the brakes. The neighbors were all gathered in a knot in front of Maggie's house, staring at Lucille Stanley's house, which—Gretchen had to blink twice to make sure she wasn't dreaming—was now painted an ugly dark mustardy yellow-green. She parked on the street, climbed out of her car, and walked over to Maggie.

"Is that ugly or what?" Maggie said in a flat voice.

Lisa, standing next to her, shook her head. "It's more than ugly. It's almost obscene."

"Does Lucille know what color her house is now?" Gretchen asked.

"We don't know," Chet said. "We're debating about who's going to tell her."

Gretchen caught his eye. "Oh, she *must* know. After all, she hired the painters."

"Lucille must really hate the neighbors to do this to us!" Maggie said in disgust.

While they stood talking on Maggie's front lawn, Dorothy Hogan pulled up in her white Toyota Celica and rolled down her window. "What an eyesore!" she gasped.

Maggie sped over. "I'm going to take her to court. Lucille took that neighborhood fund money and did this," she grumbled. "I'm going to sue her for stealing my money."

Holly stared at Maggie. "Oh, God, I wish you would stop suing everybody!"

Maggie spun around and snapped her mouth shut.

"Yes," Katalie echoed. "Stop with the suing already! It's Lucille's house. She hasn't broken any laws."

"Maybe not, but you don't live across the street from her," Maggie shouted.

Gretchen stepped forward. "Hold on a minute. Katalie's right, it *is* her house. She listened to our objections about the chartreuse color, and she did re-paint it. Maybe we don't like the new color, but it looks like Lucille does. I don't think there's anything we can do about it."

All the neighbors assembled on Maggie's lawn stared at her. Nobody said a word, and finally Gretchen marched over to her car, drove into the garage, and closed the door.

\*   \*   \*

That evening when Jarrod got home from work he found Gretchen in the living room, peering out through the window blinds. "Wow, honey, it's worse than you said on the phone." He gave her a hug.

"Oh, Jarrod, it's really, really awful. This afternoon when I got home from the hairdresser's the neighbors were all gathered in front of Maggie's house, and Maggie was threatening to sue. So I'm afraid I made a speech about minding our own business. But I can't seem to stop staring at that house."

"You're absolutely right," he said. "It is awful. But the fact of the matter is, Lucille painted her house, and then after the neighbors raised a fuss, she re-painted it. I'm not about to ask her to re-paint it again!"

Gretchen nodded.

"And here's some more interesting news that should take your mind off Lucille's house. When I drove up just now, Dorothy and Reilly Hogan were out front, yelling at poor Holly. She was just standing there on the sidewalk on her crutches, and Dorothy walked up and called her a tart."

Gretchen gasped, and Jarrod just shook his head. "Reilly told me last week that Holly made the whole thing up about him trying to kiss her. He said Holly is ruining his marriage, and he's going to make her pay for it."

"What does that mean, do you think?"

"I think he means he's going to take her to court so he can avoid paying her medical bills."

Gretchen stared at her husband. "Doesn't Reilly remember that you were also on that hunting trip? That you saw the whole thing?"

"I think he's so steamed up he's forgotten that part."

"Well, maybe you should refresh his memory!"

When the doorbell rang, Gretchen considered not opening it. "I'll get it, Jarrod said.

Reilly was standing on the porch, his hands stuffed in his pockets. "Can I come in?"

"Sure, Reilly. What's up?"

Jarrod got no farther than the stairs to the living room when Reilly's voice stopped him. "What are we going to do about that little flirt Holly Winston?"

"We? *'We'* aren't going to do anything."

"Hey," Reilly shouted. "I thought you were on my side!"

"Your side?" Jarrod said calmly. "I'm on nobody's side. I'm on the side of doing what's right."

"Well, I'll be damned."

"And another thing while we're on the subject of Holly," Jarrod continued. "If Holly needs a witness about what actually happened on that hunting trip, I will stand up for her."

Without a word, Reilly stomped back down the stairs and slammed the front door behind him.

Jarrod reappeared in the kitchen. "Wow, Gretchen, the color of Lucille's house pales in light of this fiasco with Holly."

When another knock sounded at the front door, Jarrod

groaned, so Gretchen answered it. "Holly! What brings you here?"

The girl stood uncertainly on the porch. "I waited for Reilly to leave. Is it okay for me to be here?"

"Of course it is. Come on in."

Holly adjusted her crutches and fumbled in her purse. "I wanted to show you these papers. I have a court date for my suit for damages against Reilly. I haven't given him his summons yet, and now I'm afraid to. He didn't see me coming down the street, but I overheard something that really scared me."

"Oh? What?"

"He said 'I own rifles, and I know how to use them.'"

"You mean he threatened you?"

"Well, not directly. I was standing where he didn't see me, and he was mumbling to himself. Do you think I should be worried?"

\*   \*   \*

As dinnertime drew near, Jarrod came to stand near Gretchen in the kitchen and gave her a hug. "How about minding our own business over dinner at Maria's Kitchen?"

She laughed and hugged him back.

At the restaurant, Gretchen didn't feel much like talking, and neither did Jarrod. They ate their spaghetti Bolognese in silence, and by the time they had finished their second cup of coffee, they felt somewhat better. It didn't last long.

When they drove home, they saw that the motorcycle gang was back, revving their engines in front of the Stanley's garage. Jarrod pulled into the driveway, and he and Gretchen sat watching them.

"They sure are an odd looking bunch," Jarrod remarked.

"But what are they up to? That's what I want to know."

"Looks like they're putting up a picket fence around Lucille Stanley's front yard."

"A picket fence? Why on earth would Lucille want a picket fence around her front yard?"

"I dunno, honey. But they're painting it the same color as the house."

They stared at each other, then at the fence. And, Gretchen

noted, they weren't the only ones. Maggie was pacing up and down on the sidewalk, and Gladys--good old reliable Gladys, clipboard and all--was huddled under the lilac bush by their mailbox.

Chapter Twenty-eight

# **Birds Flock Together**

The next morning, Gretchen woke up with a headache. Every time she turned around it seemed like something new was happening, and the neighborhood commotion was getting on her nerves.

"Jarrod, could you get me some Advil?" she called from the bed.

"Sure thing." He walked into the living room, and Gretchen heard him open the blinds. The next thing she heard was his voice, shouting "Holy crap! Gretchen you have to see this!"

Holding one hand to her temple, she tied her robe and walked to the living room window. "This better be worth getting out bed for."

"You better take this first." He handed her the Advil and a glass of water. She swallowed the pills, then looked across the street.

"Oh, my God!" she stammered. "Is that a pig in the Stanley's front yard? And are . . . are those chickens?" She counted five chickens and a potbelly pig. And, she noted with a groan, they were penned in a fenced area that was painted the same hideous yellow-green color as the house.

"Jarrod, is this neighborhood zoned for farm animals?"

He shook his head. "I don't think so."

She looked closer and gave a little gasp. "All those chickens have collars on! And so does the pig! Why on earth . . . ? Jarrod, we can't live across the street from *that*."

He gave her a hug. "It'll be all right, honey. We'll figure out something."

She peered out the window again. "And there's Gladys, back at her post with her binoculars trained on the Stanley's house. It's seven o'clock in the morning, and she's writing feverishly! Doesn't that woman ever sleep?"

When the doorbell rang, Gretchen was massaging her temples and Jarrod was starting the coffee. "I'm not in the mood to see anyone," she said. But she did lean over the banister when Jarrod opened the door downstairs.

"Dorothy! Good morning. What brings you out so early? It's only seven o'clock."

Without a word, Dorothy pivoted and pointed to the Stanley's house. "Reilly has gone a little nuts, Jarrod. He keeps saying he's got a rifle and he knows how to use it, and I'm afraid he'll shoot some of those chickens. Could you come over and talk some sense into him?"

There was a long silence, and then Gretchen heard her husband cough. "After last night, I'm the last person Reilly would listen to," he said.

Dorothy frowned. "What happened last night?"

"He didn't tell you about coming over here, talking about suing Holly Winston?"

"No, he didn't. What did he say?"

Jarrod coughed again. "Well, he said some pretty disparaging things about Holly, and Holly was suing Reilly for her medical expenses. I told him I'd be a witness for Holly, and he wasn't very happy about it."

Dorothy huffed out a strangled laugh. "This isn't the first time something like this has happened," she said. "I'm sick and tired of Reilly's roaming eye. I told him to just pay up and let's move on with our life."

Gretchen walked halfway down the stairs, then caught sight of Darrell and Marie Levine, Chet Gaines, and Lisa and Eli walking up their driveway. They were all still in their bathrobes! Except for Maggie, of course, who was immaculately groomed without a hair out of place, wearing a black silk blouse, cream colored slacks, and black high heels. *Looks like Maggie doesn't ever sleep, either.*

"Do you see those chickens?" Maggie demanded, her voice hard. "Do you see the *collars* on those chickens?"

Darrell let out a laugh and made a clucking sound. Marie slapped his arm. "Stop that! This is not funny!"

"Since when do chickens wear collars?" Maggie continued. "Those animals aren't dogs, they're *chickens*, for god's sake."

"I didn't need this," Jarrod growled. "I haven't even had any coffee yet."

"Neither have I," Maggie snapped. She brushed past him and stomped up the stairs. "Oh!" she said when she met Gretchen. "You're up."

Gretchen tightened her robe. "I have a headache."

Maggie ignored her, turned back, and called out the open door, "Come on up, everybody. Let's have a neighborhood meeting."

Gretchen opened her mouth to object, but Maggie was already marching into her kitchen. "I'll pour you all some coffee and put on another pot for Gretchen. Gretchen, you just sit on the sofa and get rid of your headache."

Jarrod came to life. "Hold on a minute, Maggie. We just woke up!"

"So did we!" Darrell and Chet said together. They all trooped up the stairs into the living room, and then out of nowhere, in walked Gladys. "A neighborhood meeting, is that it? I'll take notes." She withdrew the pen she'd stuck in her grey bun, moved her binoculars out of the way, and flipped over a page on her clipboard.

Gretchen folded her arms. "I don't think we need notes. This is like a scene from one of my nightmares. The only thing missing is the chickens running around my living room!"

"Well, it *is* a nightmare," Maggie pointed out. "We have a problem. Our neighborhood is not zoned for . . . chickens."

"Or for pigs," Jarrod added.

"Agreed." Maggie smiled at him. "I've already called my attorney."

"Oh, I don't think we need an attorney," Marie blurted. "Maggie, you're always so quick to sue people."

"Now, look, folks," Reilly began. "I have a rifle, and . . ."

Jarrod held up his hand. "No! We don't want to shoot any chickens. It's against the law."

Reilly narrowed his eyes, but he kept quiet.

"However," Jarrod continued, "we might have a problem with the Stanleys keeping chickens in their front yard."

"Maybe we should just go over to Lucille's," Chet proposed. "You know, talk some sense into her."

"We could do it right now!" Gladys announced. She didn't look up, just continued scribbling on her clipboard.

Eli stood up. "Yeah, let's do that. We live next door to the Stanleys. I don't want to put up with all that cackling."

"Maybe," Jarrod suggested, "Lucille could put the chickens in her backyard instead of right out on her front lawn."

"Hey, wait a minute!" Lisa said, getting red in the face. "Lucille's backyard is connected to *our* backyard."

Gladys said nothing, just continued writing.

All at once Gretchen had had enough. *Are these people really sitting in my living room at 7:30 in the morning, arguing about the neighbor's chickens? Or is this another nightmare?*

She stood up. "I want everybody's attention," she said loudly. She clapped her hands, and everyone looked up. "I am willing to talk with all of you *after* I have gotten dressed. But this is my Saturday, and on Saturday I always read the newspaper and have a cup of coffee before I do anything else. Today is no different. So if you will excuse me and my husband, we will see you all out, and later we will meet out in front of our house, say around ten-thirty."

There was a long, long silence. Then, one by one, they all got up and walked down the stairs and out the front door. When the last person had gone, Jarrod looked at her. "Wow, Gretchen, that was brilliant!"

"I'm not feeling brilliant, I can tell you. I'm going back to bed. With any luck, before we see any of the neighbors again, they will have already spoken to Lucille and this pig and chicken problem will be resolved."

*     *     *

At precisely 10:30, the neighbors reassembled in Gretchen and Jarrod's driveway. This time everyone was dressed. Lucille was across the street in her front yard, feeding the chickens and her potbelly pig. "What are you all up to?" she called.

Everyone turned to stare at her. "Lucille," Darrell yelled, "what do you think you're doing, bringing farm animals into our neighborhood?"

Gretchen touched his arm. "Darrell," she said, her voice quiet, "shut up." Then she made her way across the street and stood in front of Lucille Stanley.

"Lucille," she said calmly.

"Hi, Gretchen. Have you seen my darling chickens?"

"Yes, we've all seen them. And also your little potbelly pig. They're very cute, Lucille."

"I just couldn't resist— "

"Lucille, did you get a zoning permit for them?"

Lucille looked startled. "No, why?"

"I don't think you can keep farm animals in the city limits."

"Really?"

"Really," Gretchen said.

Lucille chewed on her bottom lip. "What do you think I should do?"

"I think you should go down to City Hall and find out whether you can keep chickens and a pig in your front yard. Maybe you can keep them in the backyard. You could build a chicken coop back there."

Lucille's expression brightened. "Oh, what a good idea! I've already named the chickens, you know."

Gretchen clamped her teeth together and managed not to laugh. *Named the chickens? She named the chickens?*

"And the pig," Lucille added. "I named the pig Robin Hood. After all," she said with a grin, "we do live in Sherwood Forest."

Chapter Twenty-nine

## Do You Hear What I Hear?

"Jarrod, do you hear motorcycles?"

He got up from the kitchen table and went to the window. "Oh, wow. They're back, the whole gang of them."

"What are they doing?"

"Well . . ." Her husband suddenly chuckled. "One of them has a big roll of chicken wire, and the guy in back of him has some two-by-fours and a toolbox tied on the back of his cycle. Looks like they're going to build a chicken coop."

"In the back yard, I hope."

"Don't know. And there's Gladys," he said. "Right on time. She doesn't miss a thing, does she?"

"There's something about that woman we're all missing," Gretchen murmured. She joined Jarrod at the window just as another motorcycle turned onto their street. She counted twelve of the noisy things, all parked in front of the Stanley's house. All the riders wore leather jackets with skulls and crossbones on the back. Some had bandanas tied on their heads, and some wore black helmets. And all of them had tattoos covering their necks and arms.

The last motorcycle to arrive had a bulky cage balanced in front of the rider. Gretchen squinted for a closer look. "Oh, my God, it's a rooster!"

Jarrod chuckled. "And there's Gladys, laughing so hard she can barely write on her clipboard!"

Gladys suddenly looked up at Gretchen and Jarrod in the window and waved. Gretchen ducked out of sight. "I have to go to the post office, Jarrod. I need to mail a package and we're out of stamps."

"Get some stamps with a chicken on them," he joked.

*   *   *

The post office on Admiral Lane was one street past the mini-mall in an old brown building with little available parking. When she pushed open the glass entry door, she groaned. The line of people waiting circled the entire room. "This is going to take a while," she said under her breath.

But she was surprised to see Maggie about ten people ahead of her, dressed in a long-sleeved orange button-down top tucked into sleek brown slacks. She was clutching two oversized envelopes in her hand. Gretchen craned her neck to read the addressee. Thad McFinley, Bankruptcy Attorney.

*Bankruptcy!* Why on earth would Maggie need . . . ?

The line shuffled forward a few feet, and all at once Maggie turned her head and spotted her. "Oh, hello, Gretchen." She walked back to speak to her. "Would you look at this line? We'll be here until dinnertime!"

Gretchen couldn't help but glance at the envelopes Maggie was holding. Maggie noticed and stepped closer, then lowered her voice. "We're . . . um . . . we're filing for bankruptcy." Her voice shook.

"Maggie, what do you mean?"

"We're running out of money. We've borrowed as much as we could on the house, and we don't know what to do anymore.

We might lose our home."

"Lose it!" Gretchen gasped. "But you and Chet . . ." Her voice trailed off.

"Chet did really well for a few years, but he hasn't worked since the recession, when he was laid off."

Gretchen touched Maggie's shoulder. "Oh, Maggie, I am so sorry."

"Please, don't tell any of the neighbors! Please! We're so embarrassed. That's why we're suing Holly Winston, and it's the reason we sued Dorothy and Reilly when Chet got shot in the behind."

Gretchen stared at her. "You mean you sue people just for the money?"

Maggie nodded. "We're really desperate."

"You know, that lawsuit against Dorothy and Reilly almost broke up their marriage!"

"I know," Maggie said sadly.

Gretchen stood in line with her package and watched Maggie walk out of the post office. As annoying as Maggie could be at times, she felt truly sorry for her troubles. It must be awful to worry that you might lose your house. Where would they go?

She was so distracted she didn't hear the postal clerk's voice.

"Next?" he said a second time.

The man behind her tapped her on the shoulder. "Lady, wake up. It's your turn."

All the way home she thought about poor Maggie. She had just turned the corner onto Sir Richard Road when she spotted a burly man in a black motorcycle jacket weaving along the sidewalk. She had to blink twice to see why.

Five chickens were strutting along in front of him on leashes. Oh for heaven's sake, he was walking Lucille's chickens! He kept tossing grain out in front to keep them moving.

She blinked and pulled into her driveway. Some of the neighbors had gathered on Lisa Fontaine's lawn, and Gretchen could see that Lisa was crying.

Then another motorcycle guy emerged from Lucille's backyard with the potbelly pig on a leash.

"Oh, boy," she muttered. "Now I've seen everything." She climbed out of the car and walked over.

Lisa had her head on Marie's shoulder. "There's a rooster," she sobbed. "And it crows all the time. It just woke my kids up from their nap!"

"This is surreal," Gretchen said. She watched for a moment, then turned away just as Lucille Stanley walked over to join them.

"Aren't my chickens cute?" she said with a grin.

Nobody said a word.

Chapter Thirty

## I Heard It at the Bookstore

Early Sunday morning, before it was even light outside, Gretchen's eyes suddenly popped open. "Jarrod, did you hear that?"

"Hear what?" he said, his voice groggy.

"That rooster! Listen . . . there it is again."

"Awful sound, isn't it?" He yawned and rolled over.

"Jarrod, it's four o'clock in the morning!" When he didn't answer, she climbed out of bed, grabbed her robe, and walked to the front window.

Two doors down, the lights in the Fontaine house were on. "Oh, gosh, I'll bet that rooster woke up Lisa's baby again." She had just started to go back to bed when she saw a movement in her front yard. Good Lord, there was Gladys in her fuzzy fur hat, hunkered down next to the mailbox with her binoculars trained on the Stanley backyard. And standing right behind her was Maggie, fully dressed, with her cell phone in her hand!

*Those women must sleep in their clothes!*

When she slipped back into bed, Jarrod opened his eyes. "Gladys and Maggie are standing out front by our mailbox," she said.

"They're both nuts," he said. "Completely nuts." In the next minute he was snoring.

"I'm glad one of us can sleep," she muttered. She snuggled back under the covers, but almost instantly she heard someone tapping at the front door.

"Oh, no," she groaned. "What time is it?" Her bedside clock read 6 a.m.

The tapping continued. Yawning, she got back out of bed, pulled on her robe again, and went to see who was at the door.

*I don't believe this.*

On the porch stood Reilly, Chet, Darrell Levine, and Lisa's husband, Eli Fontaine. Behind them, strung down the porch steps, were Maggie, Dorothy Hogan, Lisa Fontaine, and the two sleepy-eyed Fontaine children.

"What are you all doing here?"

"Didn't you hear that rooster crow this morning?" Lisa said.

"Yes, I did. It woke me up at four o'clock."

"It woke us all up, too!" Maggie responded. "You have to stop this!"

Gretchen blinked. "Me? Why me? I'm not the neighborhood police."

"No, but Lucille listens to you."

Gretchen stared at her. "Lucille obviously does *not* listen to me. After we complained about the chickens, she turned right around and got that rooster!"

"We need to have a conference about this right now," Maggie announced. She lifted a big thermos in one hand and a bakery box of pastries in the other, shouldered her way past Gretchen, and walked up the stairs to the kitchen.

Gretchen's mouth fell open. "Hold it! It's six o'clock on Sunday morning," she said loudly. "Go home, all of you!" She was pointing to the front door when she spied Gladys.

"I see we're having another neighborhood meeting," the grey-haired woman said cheerfully.

"No, we are not," Gretchen said flatly.

"We're not?"

"No. Most definitely we are not."

"Then," Maggie said in an airy tone, "we'll all meet later, say at half-past ten."

"At *your* house," Gretchen said. "Not at this house."

The minute they all trooped out, Gretchen walked into the bedroom and woke up Jarrod.

"Let's go out to breakfast."

"Mmmmmph," he muttered.

"*Now*, Jarrod. Before it gets any later."

He sat up. "What's the big rush?"

"The neighbors! That's what the big rush is about—these nutty neighbors of ours!"

\* \* \*

They drove to Strudel Bakery, where a perky waitress in a white uniform and red-checked apron took their order. "I'll have coffee and the scrambled egg plate," Gretchen said.

Jarrod nodded. "I'll have the same."

The waitress giggled.

Gretchen frowned. "What's so funny?"

"Oh, it's not you two," the waitress assured her. "An older woman came in this morning with a rooster on a leash, and she ordered the same thing for him! Can you believe it? She said he was a therapy rooster!"

"Therapy rooster?" Jarrod murmured. "Now I've heard everything."

They dawdled over breakfast, and when they finished their second cup of coffee, Jarrod leaned over and asked, "What time is it?"

"Ten. Let's hope the neighbors are meeting without us."

"Let's go to the bookstore, Jarrod."

"*You* go to the bookstore, honey. I want to go to the hardware store."

She watched him swing on down the sidewalk, then pushed open the door to Shellville Books. No one was at the cash register, so she walked to the back of the store and stopped in the cookbook section. She had just reached for a copy of "Gourmet Dining for Two" when she overheard a familiar voice in the next aisle. Two voices, she amended. Sandra Livingston's and another woman's.

She edged closer. Yikes, it was Gladys!

"Oh, Sandra, you have to put that in the book!" Gretchen heard the sound of pages being riffled. "It was so funny when the rooster arrived," Gladys continued. "And all the neighbors were woken up this morning before dawn."

"Maggie Gaines wanted to get Mrs. O'Malley to do something about it. The neighbors call Gretchen 'the voice of reason'."

"Well," Sandra said, "*is* she?"

"Oh, I don't know," Gladys said. "Who could be reasonable when chickens and a potbellied pig and a whole motorcycle gang turn up? And Lucille Stanley puts collars on a bunch of chickens and then one of those guys in a leather jacket with tattoos all over him walks a flock of them down the sidewalk! It was just too funny."

"I can't wait to finish writing my book," Sandra said. "It started off to be about the town of Shellville, but your neighborhood is so wacky I decided to just write about it."

Gretchen froze. *Sandra is writing a book about our neighborhood?*

"And guess what else?" Gladys said, her voice gleeful. "Maggie Gaines has one of those new watches that can tape things. She actually taped Lucille Stanley putting collars on all those chickens, and I almost peed my pants watching it."

"Gladys, with your notes and Maggie's tapes, we might have a bestseller!"

Gretchen fled to the front of the store and was just about to leave when a flyer caught her eye. A photograph of Sandra Livingston filled one corner, and in the other was printed "Soon to be released!" Splashed across the bottom in large boldface type was "THE NEIGHBORHOOD, A NOVEL BY SANDRA LIVINGSTON."

She found Jarrod at the hardware store, browsing in the

fishing tackle aisle. He looked up from a box of lures. "Honey, how come you're out of breath?"

"I just overheard Sandra Livingston, the bookstore owner, and Gladys Perkins talking about the book Sandra is writing. It's about our neighborhood! It's all about us—you, me, Maggie, Chet, everyone . . . even the motorcycle guys and the chickens and the rooster!"

"Wow," he said. "A book, huh?"

"Gladys has been taking notes on everything that's been happening and feeding them to Sandra. That's what that woman has been up to all these months with her binoculars and her clipboard!"

Jarrod rattled the box of fishing lures. "Well, that figures. She's certainly been getting an eyeful."

"Jarrod, do you think we should warn the neighbors?"

"Nah," he said with a laugh. "What would be the point? It's a free country. Sandra can write whatever she wants."

Gretchen said nothing, just pressed her hand over her eyes. "I feel the worst headache coming on."

Chapter Thirty-one

# From the Rear View Mirror

They drove slowly home along Robin Hood Boulevard. Feeling calmer after pancakes, scrambled eggs, and bacon, Gretchen was trying to decide how she would spend the rest of their Sunday afternoon when Jarrod turned onto Sir Richard Road. Suddenly he brought the car to a stop. "Honey, look! Everybody's sitting on lawn chairs in our driveway. I wonder what's going on?"

Gretchen gritted her teeth. "Keep driving, Jarrod. Please."

"What? Don't you want to find out what's happening?"

"No," she said firmly, shaking her head. "I don't want to know. It's just one crazy thing after another, and I *don't* want to know. It's exhausting."

Jarrod looked over at her with concern. "Gosh, I thought I was the only one feeling like we're living in a weird movie."

"I mean it, Jarrod. Keep driving. I don't want to hear about Maggie's tiara or her mother's tea-party china. I don't want anyone with binoculars watching everything that's going on. I'm tired of motorcycle gangs and chickens on leashes. I'm tired of all of it!"

"Yeah," he said, his voice quiet. "I know what you mean. This looked like such a nice, quiet neighborhood when we moved in."

Gretchen put her hand on his arm. "Keep driving, honey."

He drove around the cul-de-sac, past their house, to the corner. "You sure, Gretchen?"

She glanced back at their house and gritted her teeth. "Look. There's Gladys behind our lilac bush, writing on that darn clipboard. Of course I'm sure! I don't want to go home."

He turned off Sir Richard Road, headed for Robin Hood Boulevard, and then drove on out of town. Gretchen did not look back. When they reached Highway 30, he slowed the car.

"Which way do you want to go?"

"A couple of weeks ago I saw this really cute place for sale in the country. You want to see it?"

He looked at her out of the corner of his eye. "I guess so. Doesn't hurt to look."

In the quiet little town of Mayfield, just a few miles off the highway, Gretchen spotted a post office, a Val's grocery store, and a mini-mall with a bookstore and Tracy's Bakery.

"Take a right at that yellow two-story house with the flagpole out front."

Another right-hand turn brought them to a pretty, tree-shaded street with quaint older homes painted white or cream or a pale pastel color. All the yards had white picket fences.

Jarrod drove to the end of the street and stopped. "Where to now?"

At the end of one driveway was a big cream-colored house with white trim and a porch that wrapped all the way across the front. Two rocking chairs sat overlooking a huge expanse of green grass.

"Isn't that pretty," Gretchen murmured.

"Yeah. Looks real peaceful, doesn't it?"

"See that For Sale sign by the maple tree in the front yard?"

"Sure do," he said. "Looks like there's an open house today."

They were about to knock on the beveled glass front door when the realtor stepped out. "Oh, hello!" She smiled at Gretchen. "It's you again. Why don't you come on in?"

Jarrod's eyebrows went up and he put his hand on Gretchen arm. "How many times have you been here?" he whispered.

"Four."

"Four!"

She sent him a tentative smile. "You always said I was the most thorough woman you'd ever known."

He grinned. "Right. That's one big reason why I married you!"

*     *     *

That evening, when Gretchen started dinner, Jarrod disappeared into his workshop. An hour later he sneaked up behind her while she was sautéing mushrooms for the hamburgers.

"Remember the night I asked you to marry me?" he asked.

Gretchen turned away from the stove and smiled at him. "Oh, yes, I do, Jarrod. I'll never forget that night. You took me to dinner at that really fancy restaurant, and you got down on one knee."

"Oh, yeah," he said.

"And then you surprised me with that wooden plaque you made, the one you'd burned "Love of My Life" on.

He gave her a long look. "Here's something else I made for you." From behind his back he took something wrapped in a towel and handed it to her.

It was another wooden plaque with the words "Home Is Where We Are."

"Oh, Jarrod, I love this!" She wound her arms around his neck and kissed him. "Where should we put it?"

He hesitated so long she felt her throat tighten. When he finally spoke, his voice was hesitant. "How about over the front door of that house we looked at in Mayfield?"

"Oh, yes, Jarrod!" She kissed him again. "I was afraid you'd never ask!"

*The Neighborhood*

*Six Months Later . . .*

On a beautiful, sunny morning six months after they moved into their new neighborhood, Jarrod and Gretchen sat sipping coffee on their wide front porch. "Honey," Jarrod said with a grin, "you seem so much more relaxed since we moved in here."

Gretchen sighed happily. "Oh, yes. This new neighborhood seems really nice. It's quiet and peaceful, and nothing crazy is happening."

"Yeah. All that commotion in our old place really got to me. I'm glad we moved."

*       *       *

Early the next morning Gretchen was unloading bags from her car when she heard shouting. She looked up to see the twin boys from next door tearing down the street, chasing a strange-looking animal.

"That's our pet llama, Mrs. O'Malley!" Kyle yelled as he raced past.

*A llama! Who on earth keeps a pet llama?*

"She's learned how to unlatch our gate," Kyle's twin brother Marc shouted. "Better hide your groceries! Her name's Dina, and she likes broccoli!"

*Broccoli! A llama who likes broccoli!*

Gretchen pressed against her car door and watched Kyle and Marc trying to corral the animal. "She wanders all over the neighborhood," Kyle shouted. He slowed to a stop by her front fender. "And that's not all, Mrs. O'Malley."

*Oh, no, not more nutty neighborhood stuff!* "Oh?" Gretchen said warily.

"Heck, no," Kyle went on. "This morning, Mrs. Kent . . . you know Mrs. Kent?"

Gretchen shook her head. She was being very cautious about the people in their new neighborhood.

"Mrs. Kent lives on the other side of your bushes there. Anyway, this morning Mrs. Kent found Dina in her kitchen, licking the icing off a cake she'd just made. By the time she heard the noise in her kitchen, it was a real mess!"

*A real mess*, Gretchen thought, with a hitch in her breathing.

A llama licking cake icing in her neighbor's kitchen. You don't suppose . . .

No, that would be too unlikely, moving into a neighborhood with the same kind of crazy goings-on as their old neighborhood. Just too unlikely.

*Wouldn't it?*

THE END